Foal Play

Foal Play

Kathryn O'Sullivan

Minotaur Books

A THOMAS DUNNE BOOK

A THOMAS DUNNE BOOK FOR MINOTAUR BOOKS.
An imprint of St. Martin's Publishing Group.

FOAL PLAY. Copyright © 2013 by Kathryn O'Sullivan. All rights reserved. Printed in the United States of America. For information, address St. Martin's Press, 175 Fifth Avenue, New York, N.Y. 10010.

www.thomasdunnebooks.com
www.minotaurbooks.com

ISBN 978-1-250-02659-0 (hardcover)
ISBN 978-1-250-02660-6 (e-book)

Minotaur books may be purchased for educational, business, or promotional use. For information on bulk purchases, please contact Macmillan Corporate and Premium Sales Department at 1-800-221-7945 extension 5442 or write specialmarkets@macmillan.com.

First Edition: May 2013

10 9 8 7 6 5 4 3 2 1

For my husband and parents with love

Acknowledgments

As with many creative endeavors, this book is the result of help and support from numerous people. Thanks to my husband, who is always my first reader, kindest critic, and greatest support; to my parents, two talented writers who set the bar high and helped me reach it; and to the rest of my family, friends, and my colleagues at Northern Virginia Community College for providing me with the warmth and encouragement every writer should have.

Sincere thanks to Katy Moore for reading and believing in this novel, the amazing volunteers and organizers of the Malice Domestic conference, and everyone involved with the Minotaur Books/Malice Domestic Best First Traditional Mystery Novel competition, without whom this book would not be.

A very special thanks and deepest gratitude to my editor, Toni

Plummer, for her brilliant insights and suggestions that truly made this novel better.

Thank you to John Morrone, the copy editor who carefully reviewed every line.

Thank you to Daniel Steven for his advice.

Fond thanks to Carole Bellacera, Linda Rodriguez, Jeffrey Stepakoff, and Noreen Wald, remarkable writers and people, who took time away from their own work to read mine.

Thanks to the members of Sisters in Crime, especially those of the Chesapeake Chapter, and Margery Flax and the members of Mystery Writers of America, who inspire me with their stories, humor, and undying love of mysteries.

Sincere thanks to all those dedicated to protecting the beautiful wild horses depicted in this book.

Finally, a heartfelt thank-you to the men and women firefighters of Corolla Fire and Rescue, who so generously gave me their time and instilled in me a deep and lasting appreciation for the nobility and selflessness of firefighters everywhere.

Foal Play

Prologue

As a lazy July sun rose over the Atlantic Ocean, a lone gray and white seagull flew toward the pristine sands of the Outer Banks of North Carolina. The gull soared above softly undulating ocean swells, past dolphins leaping playfully from the sea, and over misty, breaking waves before reaching shore.

The seagull scanned the beach for its morning meal, spied a crab flinging granules from its hole, and glided low. The crab stopped its work and peeked cautiously up at the bird. The gull hovered above the crab and then, catching the scent of a tastier meal down the beach, beat its wings and sailed away toward breakfast.

The gull approached its meal, a dark form that lay partially submerged in a shallow saltwater pool created by waves cutting into the dunes. The bird screeched intermittently as it soared closer . . . thirty, twenty, ten yards away. It cocked its head and lowered its feet for landing. But the descent wasn't easy. The gull wasn't the only one interested in the small pool on the beach. Dozens of birds were zeroing in on the spot. The gray and white gull pecked its way into a blanket of beating wings. It could no longer see the blackened mass in the pool but it could smell it.

Suddenly, other sounds overpowered that of the screaming gulls—the rapid thumping of approaching horses, the harsh growl of a revving engine, the primal howl of mischief-making teens. The birds cocked their heads toward the noise. Thundering down the beach at full gallop was a herd of wild horses followed by two teen boys on a dune buggy.

The boys laughed and hollered as they chased the horses at full speed along the shore. The frightened horses snorted heavily. They had managed to stay a few feet ahead of their adolescent tormenters but their fatigue was apparent. Their muscles tightened. Their mouths foamed. Their chests sweated.

One of the boys, a freckled skater type, leaned from the buggy. He held the roll bar with one hand and stretched his arm toward the flapping mane of one of the horses. The horse was just out of reach. "Get closer!" the boy yelled. His friend, the pierced and tattooed driver, gunned the engine.

The herd headed straight toward the flock of gulls feeding at the pool. One by one the birds took flight, abandoning the pool and its treasure. The skater's face flushed pink with excitement as he extended to his full length and grabbed hold of a horse's mane. The last bird snatched a black morsel in its bill and became airborne as the horses crashed through the pool.

Water sprayed up and out. The driver yanked on the steering

wheel in an attempt to avoid the pool and pulled the buggy up short. His passenger lost his grip on the horse and dune buggy, flew across the hood, and landed, with a splash, facedown in the water.

The driver laughed and whooped at the horses as they quickly disappeared down the beach. His delighted screams mixed with those of the gulls circling above. "Man, that rocked!" The driver grinned at his friend. His smile faded when he saw his friend hovering, crablike in the pool, his eyes staring at something next to him. "Man, you okay?"

The freckled boy's arms shook as his muscles tired from holding his body above the water. His breathing grew shallow as his nostrils filled with the smell of decay. His pupils widened as his mind processed what he saw partially submerged and inches away—oddly burned and bloated skin surrounding sunken eye sockets; a nose barely maintaining its grip on a face; a lipless mouth grinning up at him. The teen tried to fight it, but slowly, from deep within his gut it rose. He swallowed hard, trying to keep it down. But it came anyway. Long and loud. His scream.

Chapter 1

"Some like it hot," said the announcer on the radio.

"And some don't," said Fire Chief Colleen McCabe as she stretched across her gray metal desk in the Corolla, North Carolina, Station 6 firehouse and turned the volume down on the radio. She leaned back in her cushioned vinyl chair, switched on her desk fan, and swiveled to look out her second-floor office window at the cloudless morning sky.

Weather junkie that she was, Colleen didn't need to hear the radio announcer's Fourth of July weather report. She had checked the local radar online, the Weather Channel, and her own thermometer and barometer before leaving this morning. One thing was clear—the Outer Banks was on the verge of a record-breaking heat wave. Today, sand would burn the soft soles of children's feet as they ran from the surf to the safety of umbrellas and towels; the sun would beat on tar roads and create the illusion of thin pools of standing water; and icicles would elongate on overworked air-conditioning units.

Despite her years of experience, Colleen's heart skipped a beat and she felt a mild sense of anxiety thinking about the dangerous combination of brittle dune grass and vacationers' illegal roadside fireworks. It wasn't battling the fires that got to her; it was the anticipation of the event. Colleen used to get the same feeling before a race at college track meets. It was the waiting for the event rather than the competition itself that unnerved her. A call to the fire station had the same effect as a call to the starting blocks had had in college. Her jitters disappeared and she became focused, calm, and in her zone.

A car horn blared repeatedly outside. Colleen stood and peered out the window. A herd of wild Corolla horses slowly clopped down Whalehead Drive. Like Secret Service agents, three uniformed Lighthouse Wild Horse Preservation Society officers followed closely behind the horses, making certain tourists kept their distance. A week earlier, a fierce tropical storm had knocked down a section of the sound-to-sea fences that separated the horses from the southern, more developed sections of Corolla. Until the fences were repaired and the horses returned to the refuge, the preservation officers were responsible for protecting herds that had escaped the sanctuary from speeding cars and curious tourists.

Colleen knew the horses were safest in the refuge but it was nice seeing them wandering the island again. The last time the threatened breed of Spanish mustangs had been this far south was in 1996, before the last of them were safely relocated behind the sanctuary fences. The 12,000 acres of refuge on the northern beaches had been created after twenty horses had been killed or injured by cars on Ocean Trail Road. Colleen missed the days when the horses roamed freely but understood the critical need to protect them.

The vacationers were eagerly trying to get close to the rare Spanish mustangs and the preservation officers were determined to stop them. Colleen watched as the line of cars grew longer behind the officers and horses. A second horn sounded and then a third.

"Stay away from the horses!" Myrtle Crepe squawked at the tourists.

Myrtle Crepe was the stocky, white-haired, sixty-five-year-old head of the Lighthouse Wild Horse Preservation Society and a royal pain to everyone visiting and living in Corolla.

Colleen sighed, tied her curly brown hair back in a ponytail, and descended the firehouse stairs. Sparky, her Border collie, followed quickly behind, his nails clicking on the corrugated metal. She approached Jimmy Bartlett, who was busy supervising the men as they checked their equipment. Jimmy was Colleen's handlebar-mustached veteran captain and her most trusted colleague.

"Everything okay, Chief?" Jimmy asked.

"Just Myrtle stopping traffic again." Colleen eyed the sparkling white engine with its navy blue stripe. "She looks good, fellas," she said and exited. She folded her arms and stood in the shade of the firehouse entrance to witness Myrtle and the preservation officers in action.

"Little Bobby, stop that traffic. You're letting cars by," Myrtle said to her son.

Bobby Crepe, the second preservation officer, obediently lumbered to the middle of the street and thrust his hand at oncoming traffic. A tourist in the first car returned Bobby's gesture with one of his own.

Myrtle spotted a small girl who had left her car and was tentatively reaching out to touch a foal. Myrtle scurried forward and whacked the child's hand. Colleen winced, having once felt that smack on her own hand. Before retiring to work as a preservation officer, Myrtle had been a teacher at Colleen's elementary school. Colleen had had the misfortune of being a student in Myrtle's third-grade class.

The girl's mother leapt from her car, rushed forward, and drew her daughter away in stunned silence. The vacationers retreated to their cars, whispering outrage among themselves.

"Was that really necessary?" Nellie Byrd asked. Nellie was the third and final officer, and the well-liked owner of Nell's Gift Shop and Rentals.

"They need to know we mean business," Myrtle said.

"We want to attract members to the horse society, not drive them away."

"Are you head preservation officer?" Myrtle asked, pulling rank.

Nellie bit her lip and turned to observe the horses as they moved off the road to the nearby dunes to munch on vegetation. Colleen found it hard to believe that Myrtle and Nellie had stayed friends since childhood. The two could not have been more different. In Colleen's mind, Myrtle was a pit bull and Nellie a cocker spaniel.

"Come here, Little Bobby," Myrtle said, pointing to the ground in front of her.

Bobby lowered his arm and shuffled to the shoulder of the road. A line of cars inched past the firehouse. Angry drivers honked at Bobby as they passed.

"Myrtle Crepe is a witch!" came an irate voice from a passing car.

Edna Daisey shook her fist at Myrtle through the open driver's-side window of her car, then took off down the road.

"Why, I . . ." Myrtle said in an indignant huff.

Colleen, Nellie, and Bobby quickly averted their eyes, not wanting to meet Myrtle's gaze. All knew the tumultuous history between Myrtle Crepe and Edna Daisey and none wanted to be caught taking sides, not if they knew what was good for them.

Edna was a sturdy redhead and Myrtle's contemporary. She had been the librarian at Colleen's elementary school when Myrtle was Colleen's teacher and had ruled the library with an iron fist. Signs posted around the library read NO FOOD! NO GUM! NO TALKING! Colleen was amazed Edna had actually allowed reading. Edna had prided herself on her meticulous maintenance of the library and its collection. Myrtle's lax attitude about book due dates and mistreatment of periodicals had driven the obsessive Edna to fits, many of them in front of Colleen and her class.

It was a surprise to everyone when Myrtle and Edna agreed to work together at the Lighthouse Wild Horse Preservation Society after retirement and a surprise to none when, a few weeks later, they were at each other's throats again. One day, in an effort to "save" the Society's documents from Myrtle, Edna had secreted them in her tote bag and was leaving the office when Myrtle caught her in the act. Myrtle promptly had Edna removed from the building and the Society. Myrtle and Edna hadn't exchanged a civil word since.

"Little Bobby, stop loitering and come here!" Myrtle said, turning her displeasure on her son.

Colleen watched Bobby walk toward her. Bobby was forty, unmarried, and still living with his mother. He was as wide as he was tall, with pudgy cheeks, sparkling blue eyes, and graying hair that was cut short and parted on the side. His blue preservation society uniform was snug around his belly; his shorts rode up on his plump inner thighs; and his matching socks were stretched to just below his sunburned, dimpled knees. Colleen wondered why he let his mother dress him like that.

"Morning," Bobby said, spotting Colleen standing in the station entrance.

"Things busy today?" Colleen asked as he approached.

Bobby sighed and rolled his eyes in Myrtle's direction.

"Little Bobby!" Myrtle said, advancing toward Colleen and Bobby.

"Little Bobby," Bobby said, mimicking his mother under his breath.

"Good morning, Mrs. Crepe," Colleen said in as sweet a tone as she could muster. Since nothing else had worked, Colleen thought she'd try killing Myrtle with kindness.

"Isn't it enough you've cast a spell on the men at the station? Now you're after my son?" Myrtle protectively grabbed Bobby's hand. "Well, your charms won't work on my Little Bobby. He's a fine boy."

"Mother!" Bobby said with a hiss and yanked his hand away.

"Yes, he is, Mrs. Crepe," Colleen said, winking at the mortified Bobby.

Myrtle gave Colleen a quick head-to-toe appraisal. "A woman in her thirties not married. Humph. Believe me, your looks aren't going to last, Leenie Beanie."

Colleen's cheeks reddened. Leenie Beanie. Myrtle had a way of finding a soft spot and stomping all over it. So what if she had been the tallest and skinniest kid in her school? So what if she had been the only girl to stand in the back row for class pictures every year? She wasn't so tall or skinny now. Besides, how would Myrtle like to know what the kids had called her?

"Colleen doesn't have time for marriage," Nellie said, joining them outside the station. "She has a career."

"Careers like hers are for men," Myrtle said and snorted for emphasis.

"*I* run a business," Nellie said.

"Exactly my point."

Nellie opened her mouth to reply, then clamped it shut. The pupils of Colleen's steel blue eyes narrowed. She wanted to give Myrtle a swift kick in her elderly derriere but decided to spare Bobby the embarrassment of seeing his mother spanked in public. He had suffered enough.

"Now that the horses are safe, why don't we go help Dr. Wales," Nellie said, changing the subject. "I heard he has a new foal on the way."

"Why didn't you tell me? Nellie, if you're keeping things from me . . ."

"Like anyone could keep something from you," Nellie said a little too sweetly.

Myrtle studied Nellie a moment. "Okay then. We're off to Doc's."

Myrtle marched down the road. Nellie and Bobby followed, unhappy ducklings. Myrtle jumped into her pickup and honked loudly. Nellie jogged and Bobby waddled to catch up. Colleen cringed as Bobby wedged himself into the middle of the front seat. Before Nellie could get the passenger door closed, the pickup was moving. Nellie managed to close the door and wave to Colleen before the vehicle disappeared in a cloud of sandy dust down the road.

Colleen shook her head and walked across the driveway. She called for Sparky who, seconds later, shot out from the back of the station with an old leather shoe in his mouth. "So that's where my shoe went," Colleen said, trying to wrestle it free. "Okay, okay," she said after a brief struggle with the dog. "If you want it that badly, it's yours."

Sparky settled down to chew on the shoe. Colleen squatted next to the dog and played with his ears. The dog had been a gift from her father when her parents moved to New Orleans for work. According to her father, every decent fire chief had to have a dog. She knew the gift had more to do with her father's worries about her safety and living alone.

Colleen didn't particularly like living by herself but it beat the complications of having another person in the house. She had tried living with her college sweetheart after graduation and it had been disaster. After a year, he had popped the question. She had tearfully declined his proposal. She wasn't ready for marriage and didn't think she would be for some time. She moved out of their apartment the next day. It wasn't fair to him to stay. She could never give him the commitment he wanted. She cried for a week, sorry for the pain she had caused him, then moved back home to the Outer Banks and became a firefighter with Whalehead Fire and Rescue.

The alarm on Colleen's watch went off. Sparky jumped, dropped the shoe, and ran to her side. The Border collie knew what the beeping meant. Time for morning rounds. Colleen smiled, not knowing which of them enjoyed rounds more. For Sparky, it was a time to put his nose out the window and into the wind. For her, driving the slim barrier island was a time of reflection about her life and the island.

As she and Sparky toured the island, Colleen pondered how Corolla had changed from a rustic destination for sportsmen to a vacation retreat for northern suburbanites. She wasn't sorry to see the practical, one-story, hurricane-proof cement structures go, but she wasn't thrilled about the new estates either. She missed the miles of dune grass and wildflowers that once covered her island. And there was nothing like rounding a bend

in the road and spotting a horse with her foal in the late after-
noon sun.

Colleen scanned the road ahead, squinted at the sky, and
sighed. "Not again." Sparky cocked his head. He saw it, too. Smoke.
The brown-and-gray, billowy kind that comes from burning trees
and brush. Colleen pressed the gas pedal, flipped on her vehicle's
flashing lights, and drove toward the development of Island
Sands.

Colleen's breathing grew shallow as she neared Island Sands.
She forced herself to inhale deeply. She needed to be calm, professional. Her past confrontations with Pinky Salvatore had not
ended well.

Antonio "Pinky" Salvatore was a developer from Long Island,
New York, who had arrived in Corolla three years ago. His Island Sands was a community of opulent estates near the southern end of Corolla. The Mafia rumors made Pinky the closest
thing the area had to the criminal element. But that wasn't what
bothered Colleen. What bothered Colleen was how Pinky repeatedly ordered his men to burn debris. Nothing stopped him.
Not citations. Not fines. Not even threats to shut down construction.

Pinky's recurring violations made Colleen a frequent visitor
to his construction trailer. Colleen's visits to Pinky made Bill
Dorman, her closest friend and the Currituck County sheriff,
jealous. Bill was straightforward and sensible. He had told Colleen directly that he thought the New York developer was interested in her. She had told Bill he was being ridiculous but
she knew what he said was true. Every time she visited Pinky's

trailer, the businessman made a romantic proposition. These inevitable, unwanted propositions were why Colleen dreaded her visits.

Colleen's cell phone rang. She glanced at the number. Bill. He must have sensed she was on her way to see Pinky. She hit the ANSWER button.

"Good morning," Colleen said, smiling in anticipation of Bill's jealous warning.

"Not so good for some of us," Bill said.

"Before you get started about Pinky—"

"Mr. Salvatore isn't my concern right now. I need you to meet me on the beach at the northern end, just inside the sanctuary."

Something was wrong. Bill only referred to Pinky as Mr. Salvatore when he was speaking in his official capacity as Currituck County sheriff. "What's up?" she asked.

"You'll see when you get here," Bill said and hung up.

Colleen changed course and headed toward the northern end. She hit the button for the station on her cell phone. Pinky Salvatore would have to deal with Jimmy today. Colleen smiled picturing the disappointment on Pinky's face when he opened the door to his trailer, two glasses of champagne in hand, and found the mustached and tattooed Captain Bartlett on his doorstep instead of her.

Chapter 2

Colleen zipped up the wet sand of the restricted-access area of the northern beach. Sparky thrust his nose out the passenger window, wagged his tail, and barked at the water spraying from the tires onto his face. She spotted Bill's white government-issue SUV, detailed with a black stripe and the word "Sheriff," parked near the foot of the dunes. Bright yellow caution tape tied to metal spikes flapped in the ocean breeze. Seagulls perched atop the stakes and circled overhead.

Colleen parked next to Bill. A gull on one of the stakes screeched in protest, then settled on the hood of her vehicle to view the activity. Sparky's nose twitched out the window, catching a whiff of something potent mixed with the salty sea air. The dog let out several sharp barks of protest as Colleen forced him to remain in the car. She left the windows open and closed the door.

Bill waved Colleen over to where he and Rodney Warren,

Bill's fresh-faced deputy, stood staring at a pool of ocean water. She trudged through the sand, ducked under the tape, and approached the two men. The wind shifted and then it hit her— the distinctly awful smell of decaying animal tissue. She hoped a stray horse hadn't been killed. Colleen pulled her shirt up over her nose and mouth to keep from gagging.

"What died?" she asked, trying to keep her breathing shallow.

"Not what—who," Bill said.

Colleen raised her eyebrows in surprise. Bill stepped aside to reveal the body in the pool. Colleen slowly approached the water's edge. The water lapped at her boots as she leaned forward and shielded her eyes from the sun to get a better look. The sight of dead bodies, human or otherwise, had never bothered her. In school she had actually looked forward to dissections in biology lab. The inner workings and structures of frogs, pigs, and crawfish had all fascinated her. It was only when the class began dissecting a cat that she refused to participate. She just couldn't do it out of respect and love for Snowflake, her pet cat at the time.

Most eyes would have been drawn to the body's badly decomposed face and frozen grin, but what attracted Colleen's attention was the skin. Even though it was bloated and peeling, Colleen knew it had been burned. Pieces of what had been clothing were now one with the charred flesh. She inched forward to examine the body more closely, but just as the smell of formaldehyde had gotten to her in biology lab, the stench of decay got to her now. Colleen stepped back before the odor of the rotting flesh warming in the mid-morning sun overwhelmed her.

"Two kids found it this morning," Bill said.

"You think it was burned somewhere on the beach?" she asked, joining him upwind of the body.

"Not likely. This body was dumped or washed in."

"An accelerant, maybe gasoline," Colleen said. "When I talk to the coroner I'll have a better idea."

Bill folded his arms over his chest, glanced up the beach a moment, then turned back to Colleen.

"Look, Colleen, I called you out of protocol and professional courtesy. I don't want you interfering."

"When do I interfere?"

"When don't you?"

Rodney retreated and began taking photos of the body, an activity preferable to witnessing the confrontation between the sheriff and fire chief.

"I'll stay out of the way," Colleen said.

"I wish that were true," Bill said and gazed out at the ocean.

Colleen sighed. Okay. So maybe she had conducted some un-official investigations of Bill's cases in the past. She had only been trying to help. And if it hadn't been for her unsolicited input and discoveries she was convinced that many of his cases would have gone unsolved. Bill was good at what he did, but as far as Colleen was concerned he was too "by the book." Sometimes it was better to go with your gut.

Colleen had developed a great respect for her instincts when, at the age of eight, she had detected her babysitter's affair with her best friend's husband. The affair would probably have re-mained a secret if all parties involved hadn't lived in the same apartment building. Colleen's babysitter lived on the first floor with her two children. Directly above the babysitter lived the babysitter's lover and his wife, the babysitter's best friend. And on the floor above the babysitter's lover and his wife lived young Colleen and her parents. Given the close quarters, it hadn't taken curious Colleen long to figure out that while she and the baby-sitter's children were playing outside, the grown-ups were inside playing games of their own.

Young Colleen had had no idea that announcing the infidel-ity at a neighborhood picnic would cause such a fuss. Tears were shed. Punches were thrown. Ambulances were summoned. There had been a lot of screaming, not the least of which had been di-rected at her. Her mother and father had been furious at Colleen for not minding her own business. Did she know how hard it was for them to find a good babysitter? Colleen still didn't understand why she had been grounded. She wasn't the one who had had the affair. As far as she was concerned, if the babysitter hadn't been up to hanky-panky with her best friend's husband the whole ugly incident could have been avoided.

No, her gut had never steered her wrong and right now it was telling her that the burned body on the beach meant trouble had arrived on their little island. Bill would need all the help he could get. Perhaps a new approach was in order. Colleen gently placed a hand on her friend's shoulder.

"Come on, Bill," she said, lowering her voice. "How long have we been friends?"

Bill saw Rodney watching them and quickly pulled away. "Shouldn't you be preparing for tonight's fireworks? Checking permits, the engine, duty schedules?"

Colleen's neck and cheeks flushed red with fury. It was one thing for Bill to stubbornly protest her involvement in the case. It was another thing to tell her how to do her job. She glared at him a moment, waiting for him to take it back. Rodney pretended to study his camera. A gull squawked. An awkward moment passed.

"Fine!" Colleen snapped.

She stomped to her vehicle, where Sparky eagerly awaited release. She yanked open the driver's-side door, shooed the dog aside, squeezed in, started the engine, and hit the gas. The SUV spun its wheels in the sand, then lurched forward down the beach. Sparky watched sadly out the window as Bill and the stinky pool disappeared behind him.

Colleen returned to the firehouse in a foul mood. She pulled into the lot in the back. She pushed open the door and was nearly knocked to the ground as Sparky leapt out and hurried inside. He knew to stay clear of her when she was angry. There would be no treats, no walks, no fun.

Colleen stormed into the station. Having finished the morning chores, two of the volunteers were taking a break playing Nerf basketball. Jimmy spotted Colleen marching through the entrance and instantly sensed something was wrong. He tried to warn the men playing basketball with a quick whistle but it was too late. Colleen rounded the corner and one of the Nerf players bumped into her as he was about to take a shot.

"Sorry, Chief," the man said, recovering and preparing to shoot.

"What's going on here?" Colleen asked, grabbing the ball from the volunteer's hands.

Jimmy quickly stepped forward. "I thought the guys could use some downtime. Everything's ready for tonight."

"Inspection. Now!"

The men scrambled to attention in a line along the wall. Colleen walked the firehouse, checking for any task that still had not been performed—unswept floors, missing oxygen masks, improperly wrapped hoses. As she approached the men to inspect their appearance, they avoided eye contact. Nobody wanted Chief McCabe to interpret eye contact as a sign of disrespect or insubordination. They knew from experience that this was one thing she wouldn't tolerate.

As she studied the men's faces, Colleen remembered how lonely she had felt when she first became chief. It had been hard, especially for the older, more experienced firefighters, to adjust to the idea of having a woman for a boss. They had reluctantly accepted her as an important member of the team, even eventually as fire lieutenant, but as chief? They didn't think so.

The rebellion had come mostly in the form of the cold shoulder, clearing a room when she entered or whispering inside jokes and laughing behind her back. But there had also been the occasional sexist comment loud enough for her to hear, a lewd gesture within her line of sight, and sexually explicit pinups and calendars posted on the outside of the bathroom door. What the firefighters hadn't counted on was Colleen's Irish stubbornness and intense work ethic. The more insubordinate they became, the more Colleen dug in her heels and demanded the men be fit, professional, and sober.

The turning point had come a month into the job. She had

given the men a chance to adjust and get their act together. It was time to call a meeting and lay down the law. She had told them calmly and quietly: 1) They could bemoan the loss of their old chief and the former fraternity-type atmosphere, but it wouldn't change the present circumstances. 2) She wasn't there to be their friend—she had enough friends. 3) Her priority was safety—the community's and theirs. 4) Hard work would be recognized and rewarded. And 5) Firing someone was preferable to attending his funeral. Then she had marched from the room.

It was in the moment of silence after her departure that the men finally got it. They weren't going to break her. She wasn't going anywhere. Colleen was fire chief because she wanted to be fire chief, because she valued and respected the job, because she cared about the safety of the community and her firefighting team. As much as the men had opposed her upon her appointment, that was how loyal they were now.

Colleen felt her temperature and blood pressure return to normal as she examined the engines and men. Despite her best effort to find something wrong, the station was in tip-top shape. Jimmy clearly had the men ready for tonight. He was right; they did deserve some downtime. It wasn't fair to take out her anger at Bill on the guys.

"Put your feet up," Colleen said. The men glanced at one another, unsure. "Relax. At ease."

One by one the men fell out of line, the storm now over. Colleen tossed the Nerf basketball to the firefighter who had bumped into her and smiled.

"If you can beat Kenny, I'll make Sunday's spaghetti," she said.

"We'll hold you to that, Chief," the man said and moved to take a shot.

The guys began cheering the Nerf players and things were back to normal. Jimmy approached Colleen as the men played. "Everything okay?"

"Some kids found a body at the northern end. Bill's out there now," Colleen said, not wanting to get into what had happened between her and Bill. "So how'd it go with Pinky?"

Jimmy smiled broadly. Colleen grinned. "Champagne," they said in unison.

"So what did he say about the burning?" she asked.

"Once he saw it was me, not much. I cited him like always but fines don't mean anything to that guy. He's gonna keep it up until you go out with him, Chief."

"Ha-ha," Colleen said, playfully punching Jimmy in the arm.

"He had a new guy. Maybe an assistant. Kept lurking over my shoulder. You know the kind of person that stands too close?"

"Pinky's connected to the company doing the fireworks this year. Maybe the new guy is part of the fireworks crew." Colleen glanced at her watch. "Speaking of which, it's time to get things in gear."

"Gotcha," Jimmy said, suddenly businesslike, and whistled to get the men's attention.

As Jimmy rounded up the men, Colleen's mind drifted to this latest news about Pinky. It was bad enough she had to fend off

Pinky's advances, now she was going to have to deal with a space-invading assistant. This was news best kept from Bill . . . not that she and Bill were speaking.

"Chief?" Jimmy said.

Colleen turned and saw Jimmy and the men waiting for her orders. She'd worry about Pinky's new assistant and work things out with Bill later. Duty called.

Chapter 3

After a hearty dinner of fried chicken, potato salad, and apple pie, Colleen called everyone to order, reviewed assignments and procedures for a final time, and turned the floor over to Jimmy to lead them in firefighter A.W. "Smokey" Linn's 1958 "The Fireman's Prayer."

The men bowed their heads in reverence.

"'When I am called to duty, God,'" Jimmy began.

Colleen studied her firefighters as they silently prayed, eyes closed, lips mouthing the familiar words. She knew through private conversations that a few of the men were not particularly religious. However, they chose to participate as a show of solidarity and took the moment as an opportunity to reflect on the importance of the job and their families. Every firefighter appreciated that the next call could be his or her last.

Most stations around the country now reserved "The Fireman's

Prayer" for special occasions and posted it at the station rather than have it said at meals. Sensitive to her team's diversity of beliefs and faiths, she had put the issue to a vote shortly after she had become chief. After much thoughtful discussion, the Station 6 family had decided unanimously to have the prayer said as part of tradition and agreed that those who did not want to participate or be present were free to abstain without retribution.

Jimmy concluded and the men joined him in a final "Amen."

The men assigned to the Fourth of July fireworks packed for the short trip to the Whalehead Club grounds. The club was a favorite destination for vacationers wanting to tour the fully restored 1920s-era building with its Art Nouveau architecture. It was also adjacent to the ever-popular 162-foot-high, historic Currituck Beach Lighthouse. The grounds offered visitors a place to enjoy fireworks, summer concert series, boating, and wine and art festivals while the lighthouse afforded anyone willing to climb the 214 cast-iron steps stunning sunsets and spectacular views.

Colleen checked her own equipment, left Jimmy in charge at the station to handle calls, and proceeded to the fireworks staging area with Sparky to do a final inspection with the pyrotechnics company supervisor.

As the sky blazed pink and salmon with the setting sun, the crowd of vacationers making their way north to the Whalehead Club increased in numbers. This year, in addition to the fireworks, Beach Resort Realty was sponsoring a fair with booths, food, giveaways, and activities for children. Colleen was not happy about this. More people meant more traffic problems and more chances for something to go wrong.

Colleen waved from her window as she drove past Nellie Byrd manning the Lighthouse Wild Horse Preservation Society booth. She spotted Bill instructing people on available parking but avoided eye contact and kept driving. He could apologize to her later.

She passed throngs of people walking along the road to the fair. There were families with children, love-struck couples with blankets, young executives with cell phones, and packs of teens with mischief on their minds. She parked in an area designated for emergency vehicles and leashed Sparky, who tugged hard when she opened the door.

The smell of funnel cake, barbecued chicken, cotton candy, hot dogs, and freshly baked pies swirled together, creating an overwhelming olfactory experience. Sparky whined with pleasure. Colleen pulled the Border collie away from the booths through the crowd to the roped-off area where the fireworks would be ignited. Her assessment and approval was necessary before the show could begin.

Colleen eyed the dozen or so pyrotechnic workers in orange safety vests and searched for their supervisor. She noticed a handsome, tanned man in his early twenties with dark curly hair admiring the sunset. The man's hands were shoved into the back pockets of his jeans, giving him a stance reminiscent of a young Marlon Brando. He shifted his gaze and their eyes met. Her cheeks flushed pink at having been caught watching him and deepened to red when he smiled at her.

"Can I help you?" came a voice from behind her.

Colleen jumped and discovered the pyrotechnics supervisor

studying her. "Mr. Marchetti," she said, regaining her composure.

"In the flesh," the man said. "We've been waiting for you, Chief McCabe."

"Right," Colleen said. "Let's do this, then."

As Colleen and the supervisor moved away toward the explosives, she stole a look over her shoulder and searched for the handsome, tanned worker but there was no sign of him. She refocused her attention on the supervisor and the task of scrutinizing the site.

Colleen devoted the next thirty minutes to carefully completing the inspection. After conferring with the supervisor and ordering the removal of several defective shells, she was satisfied that the setup was in order and signed off on its safety. She scanned the crew as they positioned themselves for the start of the fireworks show, searching their faces for the worker she'd seen earlier.

"Is something wrong?" the supervisor asked.

"Is this all of your crew?"

The supervisor gave his men a once-over. "Sure is," he said after a moment. "You looking for someone?"

How could she ask the supervisor if he had a man with a tan and dark hair working for him? The description fit more than half of his crew. And what legitimate reason could she give for asking about him? She had none. "No, I'm good," Colleen said and left the supervisor and his team to do their jobs.

Colleen made her way toward her vehicle, puzzled. If the man she had seen earlier wasn't part of the fireworks team, then who was he and why was he wearing an orange vest like those of the pyrotechnic workers? Perhaps more important, why did she care? Was she actually attracted to this younger man? Ridiculous, she thought. He's not even my type.

A flash of movement near the Currituck Beach Lighthouse caught her eye and instantly caused her to forget the handsome stranger. Was there someone lurking near the historic structure? That section of the grounds had been cleared and cordoned off because of its proximity to the fireworks. If somebody was there, she needed to get them out for their own safety.

Colleen cautiously approached a cluster of pines and bushes. She peered back over her shoulder as she crept onto the lighthouse property. She was no longer visible to the fireworks crowd. Suddenly, Sparky stopped, cocked his head, and pointed his nose at the woods. She squeezed the leash tight in her hand, listened, and heard what had attracted the dog's attention—a low, deep whistle. Someone was hiding in the shadows.

Colleen and Sparky stood motionless. She eyed the thicket of trees for any sign of movement but the foliage was dense and the sunlight fading. She wished she had her sturdy metal Maglite with her for illumination and protection. Her heart beat loudly in her ears as she waited for additional noise. Nothing. Whatever she thought she had seen or heard was gone. The sound of the pines swishing in the breeze and the delighted screams of children at the fair slowly filtered their way back into her consciousness. She pulled Sparky away from the wood toward the emergency vehicle parking area.

"Colleen," came a whispered voice. Colleen whirled around and peered with concern at the grove. "Get over here this instant!" came a cranky command.

Colleen's concern swiftly became annoyance. "Myrtle? Is that you?"

"Geez, yes, just get in here."

"I'm working. Why don't you come out here," Colleen said, straining to see her former school teacher in the darkness.

"Can't. Too dangerous."

Colleen rolled her eyes. "Myrtle, you're perfectly safe. But you won't be when the fireworks start."

"Then you'd better get in here quick."

Colleen sighed. Better humor Myrtle and get her out of the restricted area before the fireworks started exploding overhead. All she needed was to have the falling embers hit the trees and Myrtle go up in flames. Colleen picked her way into the grove of trees. Sparky whimpered, excited to be exploring new territory.

"To your left," Myrtle said in a whisper.

Pinecones crunched underfoot as Colleen walked in the direction of Myrtle's voice. Sparky tugged on his leash, impatient at the slow progress. Finally, Colleen reached her former teacher. "What are you doing in here?"

"Not so loud. You want someone to hear us?" Myrtle said, grabbing Colleen's arm and yanking her deeper into the wood.

"I'm busy and the mosquitoes are biting, so what is it?" Colleen asked and pulled her arm away.

Myrtle checked to be sure they were alone. "The men who brought the fireworks? They're friends of Antonio Salvatore."

"Oh, for crying out loud, Myrtle. I don't have time to hear about Pinky right now," Colleen said in disgust and turned to go.

"Colleen Elizabeth McCabe," Myrtle said in a tone Colleen hadn't heard since she was nine years old. "You will listen to me when I'm speaking."

Colleen reluctantly faced Myrtle. "You've got ten seconds. Go."

Myrtle took a deep breath. "Earlier this evening, when I was patrolling the herds near the lighthouse, I saw three men unloading fireworks. I didn't think too much about them until one of them pulled out a gun. Then I got worried they'd shoot one of the horses grazing on the grounds."

"They went after the horses?" Colleen asked, now concerned.

"No. The gunmen didn't even seem to notice the horses, but if they had I bet they would've shot them. What kind of people have guns in Corolla? I'll tell you what kind—gangsters. Mr. Salvatore is setting up Mafia headquarters here. I just know it."

Colleen highly doubted Pinky was making Corolla Mob headquarters. She wondered if Myrtle had really seen a gun. After all, Myrtle had witnessed the event at a distance with a sixty-five-year-old's eyesight. "When was the last time you had your eyes checked?"

"I don't need glasses!" Myrtle said, raising her voice. "I know what I saw. I watch the news. I read the *Outer Banks Sentinel*. If I say I saw a gun, then I saw a gun."

Before Colleen could reply Sparky started growling. It was a low growl like the one he used when delivery persons came to the door at home. Colleen scanned the trees and saw the outline of a man advancing toward them . . . and he had a gun. She jerked

Myrtle to the ground and quietly ordered Sparky to be silent. He, too, lay down. Colleen, Myrtle, and Sparky spied as the man drew closer and peered into the thicket in their direction.

"Hey, it's Sweet Boy. . . . That you?" the man asked in a gruff whisper.

Sparky snarled; Colleen pulled him closer. The man stared into the brush that enveloped them. Colleen studied as much of his profile as she could in the dim light but all she could make out was a strong nose. The man paused a moment, then tucked the gun in the small of his back and disappeared the way he had come. Colleen, Myrtle, and Sparky waited until they were sure the coast was clear, then let out a collective sigh. Colleen found that she had been squeezing Myrtle's arm and released her.

"That's some grip you've got there," Myrtle said and rubbed her forearm.

"Sorry," Colleen said with sincerity. She had been told more than once that she had a viselike grip. She hoped Myrtle didn't bruise easily.

"Now do you believe me?" Myrtle asked.

"Did you tell anyone else about what you saw?"

"Of course not. What do you take me for?" Myrtle asked, back to her usual, crabby self.

"You should tell Sheriff Dorman. This is really his department."

"I can't. A man saw me. They've probably got me under surveillance. You tell him."

Colleen thought about her disagreement with Bill on the beach and how he had accused her of meddling. "Trust me, the sheriff will prefer talking to you."

"But if I go to the sheriff they'll whack me."

Myrtle had obviously seen one too many episodes of *The Sopranos*. The likelihood of anyone being whacked in the Outer Banks was slim to none. In the last two years there had only been one murder in all of Currituck County, not counting the body found on the beach this morning. Still, there was something disturbing about a man with a gun lurking in the woods.

"Fine," Colleen said. "I'll tell Sheriff Dorman what you saw and you can go home and be safe."

"I can't go home. Nellie's expecting me at the booth."

Maybe it was her fight with Bill this morning. Maybe it was being stuck in the mosquito-infested trees with her former teacher and a gunman. Maybe it was the heat. But Colleen had had enough. "Damn it, Myrtle, either you think someone's trying to kill you or you don't. My advice? Go home. But you do what you want!" she said with irritation.

"Well . . . I never . . . and after all I taught you," Myrtle said after a moment of shock and marched away in a snit.

Colleen groaned in frustration as Myrtle stomped through the foliage and disappeared. Sparky squirmed on his leash wanting to follow. In case Myrtle really was being watched, Colleen held back a few moments before picking her way out of the trees. Until she knew for certain what was going on, there was no point in taking any chances. The presence of the man with the gun brought back her earlier concern about trouble arriving in

Corolla. Was it coincidence or were the body on the beach and the man with the gun somehow connected? And if so, how? Colleen didn't have answers to her questions but she had every intention of getting some.

Chapter 4

*"**Never eat more** than your mask can hold."* It was one of the first lessons Colleen learned as a junior firefighter and it came to mind now as she passed fairgoers stuffing their mouths with greasy treats from vendors.

Colleen pushed her way through the crowd searching for Bill. Her heart beat in her throat and perspiration ran down her temples. She fought through the lines of people and squinted from the intensity of the lights hung around the grounds. A teen boy jostled Colleen and stepped on Sparky's paw. Sparky barked at the boy as he disappeared behind the "Dunk the Clown" cage. Colleen spotted Bill three booths away. She waved and called out to him but her voice was drowned out by the sound of the announcer on the loudspeaker broadcasting the beginning of the fireworks.

The lights around the booths dimmed. All eyes focused upward. Neon necklaces, bracelets, and anklets floated about the grounds on the bodies of children. A woman with a stroller bumped into Colleen and apologized profusely. She forced a smile, then surveyed the area for Bill. She scanned the booths, grounds, and road but he was nowhere to be seen.

The first fireworks exploded overhead. Colleen did a final search for Bill and turned back toward the engines. Her job demanded her complete attention now. She'd tell Bill about the man with the gun as soon as the fireworks were over. She concentrated on the falling debris from the explosives and began her patrol of the area with Sparky. The dog had an uncanny ability to detect fire the moment a spark ignited. It was how he had earned his nickname.

It took Colleen more than half an hour to circle the fairgrounds, during which she stopped occasionally to appreciate the fireworks. As a child her favorites had been the green and red ones that burst into enormous parachutes and the small white ones that broke apart, fragments whistling as they flew in different directions. However, after fifteen years of firefighting, she now preferred the ones that burst into stars and then quickly fizzled out.

Colleen reached the emergency vehicle parking area. The grand finale would be starting soon. She wanted to get Sparky into her SUV before the final series of fireworks were rapidly launched into the air. The loud noises had always bothered the canine. If it weren't for his expert nose, she would have left him safely locked up at the station.

Sparky pulled hard on his leash. "Hey, easy there," Colleen said in a firm voice.

The dog barked loudly. He cocked his head to the side with one ear up. Colleen followed Sparky's gaze south, away from the fireworks. Her eyebrows furrowed. Then she realized what had put him on alert. A fire.

Colleen leapt into action, her athlete's reflexes kicking in. The fireworks' grand finale began as she raced to her SUV at top speed, Sparky right beside her. She yanked open the door and Sparky jumped inside ahead of her. She whipped the door closed, started the engine, and flicked her emergency lights on. Just as she was reaching for her cell phone, it rang. She checked the number on the display. It was Jimmy. She hit the green button.

"I'm headed down Ocean Trail now," she said before Jimmy could speak.

"The call just came in. How'd you know, Chief?"

Colleen peeked at Sparky and rubbed his ears. "Sparky."

"That dog deserves a medal," Jimmy said.

"I think he'd prefer a pig's ear. See you there," Colleen said and hung up.

Colleen zipped down the two-lane highway, lights flashing and siren blaring, and heard the alarm at the firehouse sound. She would be just in front of them. She peered at the night sky and could barely make out a path of black smoke obstructing the stars. Familiar with the neighborhood, she traced the smoke path to its source. Mostly locals and vacationers interested in fishing on the sound resided there. The booms of the fireworks were fading behind her when, suddenly, there was a loud explosion up ahead. Sparky howled.

"Damn," Colleen said and stomped on the pedal. The explosion meant gas had leaked at the fire. She hoped nobody had been home at the residence.

The hot summer wind whipped through Colleen's hair. She reached into the glove compartment for an elastic to tie her tresses back. With a practiced hand she wrapped her hair in a short regulation ponytail at the nape of her neck and put on her hat. She saw the engine approaching in her rearview mirror. Good. Jimmy and the guys were right behind her.

As Colleen pulled off the main road four wild horses darted across her path in a panic. They had clearly been near the explosion and were disoriented and confused. Colleen took a second to watch them run to safety among the dunes, then steered onto a side road. As she made her way to the scene, she could feel the heat of the fire. It was only then that she realized the residence rapidly burning to the ground was that of Myrtle and Bobby Crepe. Myrtle's earlier words about the man with the gun echoed in her mind. "A man saw me. . . . If I go to the sheriff they'll whack me." The hair on the back of Colleen's neck stood on end. Was someone trying to kill Myrtle because she had seen too much? Had she been wrong to advise Myrtle to go home? Colleen swallowed hard, hoping Myrtle was still at the fair with Nellie.

Colleen screeched to a halt in the sand a safe distance from the house, ordered Sparky to stay, and slammed her door closed. Bill was already there ordering his men to secure a perimeter to keep onlookers away. The engine arrived and the firefighters jumped into action putting on masks, grabbing Halligan tools and axes, and pulling hoses.

Her first priority was to ascertain whether Myrtle and Bobby had been home and if so, to get them out, She glanced over the one-story rambler. Most of the activity was in the front left of the house. The blast had shattered windows in that section and smoke, heat, and gases billowed out and heavenward. That would save her team the task of ventilating the building. They needed to enter the structure and locate possible victims soon before it collapsed. She met Jimmy at the front of the engine.

"The search-and-rescue guys ready?" she asked.

Jimmy peeked around the side of the engine at the men donning their facepieces and breathing apparatuses. The last man secured his equipment and gave Jimmy the thumbs-up.

"Ready," Jimmy said.

Colleen nodded and Jimmy signaled the men to enter the building.

As the men made their way to the front door, curtains in another room of the house ignited in flames.

"We need to get this thing under control. Get the guys on layering the fire to protect our men. Salvage as much of the Crepe home as possible," Colleen said.

"Got it," Jimmy said and moved away to attend to the fire control and conservation duties.

Colleen listened on her walkie-talkie as her team made its way into the smoky structure. She bit the inside of her lip, a nervous habit that wouldn't subside until all were safely out of the building.

The men cranked open the hydrant and began dousing the flames, working in layers, from ground to roof, right to left, and back again. As Colleen monitored their progress, Bill joined her.

"You think anyone was home?" he asked.

"I hope not," she said with genuine concern. "See anything before I got here?"

"A broken window in front maybe. Could have been the explosion." Colleen nodded and an awkward pause followed. "Well, let me know if you need anything," Bill finally said, tipped his hat, and jogged off.

Colleen exhaled deeply. She hated when they fought.

It took a while before the men got the fire under control. Colleen surveyed the exterior of the residence. Her squad had managed to save half of the structure but the roof over the kitchen was gone and there was extensive smoke and water damage. The men had done well, all things considered. Colleen relaxed a little. Then the bad news came. The rescue team had found a body.

Her heart sank. It was an experience no firefighter wanted to have.

"Chief? You there?" said the rescue team leader over the walkie-talkie.

"I'll be right in," Colleen responded. She took a breath, donned protective gear, and proceeded toward the house.

Colleen stepped over the threshold and made her way through the remains of the foyer. The rescue team parted to let her pass. She entered the kitchen and saw the body. It was scorched beyond recognition but Colleen could tell by its size that it was the body of a woman, a stout woman. She stood in the middle of what was left of the room and shook her head in disbelief. Myrtle Crepe was dead.

She scrutinized Myrtle's charred body: hair burned from the skull; hands curled protectively over the chest; one leg bent under the torso. A horrible way to die, Colleen thought.

"Someone call the coroner. See if he's still local," Colleen said and stepped away. "And tell Bill he'll need Rodney to get pictures before we cover her," she added over her shoulder. "The coroner could be a while."

There was a brief silence, then Rodney was summoned and the team got to work. As photos were snapped, Colleen collected herself and turned her attention back to the kitchen. She still had a job to do. She owed it to Myrtle to find out what had happened.

She put her hands on her hips and eyed the layout. She remembered what Bill had said about a broken window. She walked to the window frame and felt glass crunch under her boots. Given the explosion, the glass should have been blown out. Why was there so much glass inside? Something must have been thrown in through the window. Colleen's brows furrowed as a new thought crossed her mind. Did somebody mean to start the fire? If so, that meant an arson investigation.

"Look at this," Jimmy said, motioning to a soggy pile of debris near the stove.

Colleen glanced at a fire extinguisher still in its cardboard box and sighed. She suspected that the batteries in the smoke detectors, if Myrtle even had a smoke detector, probably needed replacing. She had seen it one too many times. Lives and property lost because someone forgot to perform a simple task like changing a battery.

Colleen rubbed her forehead with the back of her hand. Perspiration dotted her face and ran down her neck and back. Her temples began to throb.

"Make notes for the report. Call me when we get word from the coroner," she said and left the kitchen.

She crept down the long corridor that served as the spine of the one-story building. Boxes of junk lined the hall. Colleen switched on her Maglite. When Mr. Crepe was alive he had added several rooms over the years, resulting in a strange, funhouselike structure. The hallway turned abruptly in places and the height of the ceiling changed, which forced Colleen to duck at times.

The floorboards creaked as she went in and out of rooms. The bedrooms at the back of the house were relatively undamaged. Colleen rolled her eyes when she saw Bobby's room decorated like a child's, complete with Mickey Mouse lamp and cartoon character wallpaper. The black-and-white bedspread, laptop computer, and biker magazines were the few adult elements. She wondered how a man his age could live like that. Then again, as far as Colleen was concerned, a forty-year-old man shouldn't be living with his mother.

The hallway ended with two doors on either side. She opened the door on the left first. Inside she found boxes, an old bicycle, a rusted beach umbrella, a tool box, bags of old clothes, yellowed magazines, and an incomplete dish set among the many items strewn about the room. Myrtle's house was a good candidate for the television show *Clean House*.

Colleen stepped across the hall and opened the final door. Myrtle Crepe's heart and soul were contained within. The room was packed with Lighthouse Wild Horse Preservation Society materials. Pictures of and newspaper articles about the wild Spanish mustangs of Currituck Beach were tacked on the walls. Copies of the Society newsletter were everywhere. A plaque and painting of Star, a stud who was killed years ago, hung on the wall above a desktop computer.

Colleen skimmed an article on the wall that had been circled in red and remembered the stir it had caused when it was published. The reporter had claimed that the horses of Corolla were not descendants of the Spanish mustangs brought to the barrier island in 1523 but rather that of common farm horses taken across the water by their owners as a way for them to escape grazing restrictions on the mainland.

After the article had come out, Myrtle and Nellie had prepared a special edition of the newsletter exclusively devoted to defending the bloodline of the mustangs. Included in it was testimony from veterinarian Doc Wales, who diplomatically pointed out that the more important issue was that the horses somehow connected people to the past. In recent years, DNA evidence had finally put the issue to rest, confirming the Corolla horses' Spanish bloodline.

Colleen was unexpectedly overcome with feelings of sadness and guilt. Myrtle was dead and it was her fault. If she hadn't ordered Myrtle home, her former teacher might still be alive. Why, for the first time in her life, had Myrtle listened to Colleen instead of remaining at the fair? For all her annoying traits—and

Colleen thought she had many—Myrtle Crepe had added color and life to the community. She was family.

She leaned against Myrtle's desk, exhausted. She picked up the whistle Myrtle had used to blow at people who got too close to the horses. She wondered how Bobby would take his mother's death. She didn't envy Bill. He would be the one who would deliver the unfortunate news.

"Chief? You back here?" Jimmy asked from down the hall.

"Yeah," Colleen said.

"Coroner called. Says it might be a few more minutes but he'll be here."

"I'll be right out," she said, wiping tears from her eyes. She made her way to the hall, took one last look around Myrtle's room, and closed the door.

Colleen paused at the kitchen entrance and stole a glimpse of the now-covered body before exiting the Crepe home. As she emerged she noticed a small crowd gathered at the perimeter. There was something about a fire that attracted people. It didn't trouble her. On the contrary, Colleen understood the fascination. When she was a child and living in an apartment complex on the mainland, there were only two things that got the neighborhood kids running—the ringing bell of the ice cream truck and the blaring siren of the fire engine. As soon as she heard the ear-splitting wail of approaching engines, she would race to the street, then sprint, first in front of, then alongside, then behind the engines. She was always faster than the other kids, including the boys. After chasing a few fires, Colleen got good at predicting where the trucks were headed and took shortcuts through playgrounds, terrace-level walkways, and storm drains, sometimes arriving just in time to see the engines pulling up.

She had cherished those rare moments when she arrived early, before the firefighters sprang into action. One time in particular, she had arrived several minutes before the firefighters, partially because of her intimate knowledge of the apartment complex and partially because the fire truck had been unexpectedly blocked down the road by a construction crew. When she realized the fire-fighters were delayed, she ran up the stairs of the building, knocked on doors, and screamed for people to get out. She even carried one family's frightened dog down the steps before the firefighters finally arrived and dragged her back from the building. Colleen would never forget the good feeling she had had in saving the dog or the pat on the back she had received from one of the firefighters.

She noticed a commotion in the crowd gathering behind the yellow perimeter tape. She spotted Bill, arms folded and feet firmly planted two feet apart. Colleen recognized this stance. It was the one he took when he felt people were being unreasonable. It was the one he had taken this morning with her.

"What's going on?" she asked Jimmy.

"Nellie's insisting on coming in."

Colleen's heart sank. Bill was breaking the bad news. She made her way toward Bill to try and help.

"We don't have an ID on the body, Nellie," Bill said, trying to reason with Myrtle's best friend. "You don't know it's her. Isn't that right, Chief McCabe?"

Colleen nodded. "The sheriff's right. We won't know if it's her until the coroner's report."

666

"She never showed at the fair. It's not like Myrtle to miss manning the booth. I know it's her," Nellie said with a sob.

Colleen knew it, too. "Sheriff Dorman or I would be happy to call you as soon as we hear," she said, gently touching Nellie's shoulder.

"Why don't you go home, Nell. We know how to reach you. And there's nothing to be done here," Bill said.

"But what about the Society documents? Myrtle kept the originals in her home office. I told her how foolish it was to keep them here, even offered to keep them in my store safe, but she wouldn't listen. All because of that thing that happened with her and Edna," Nellie said with disapproval.

Colleen's eyebrows raised in surprise. Did she detect an unusual note of anger in Nellie's voice?

Nellie caught Colleen studying her. "I'm sorry. I just can't believe she's gone," she said and sighed.

"That section of the house is relatively unharmed," Colleen said. "Once it's safe, I'd be happy to have those materials removed for safekeeping."

"How about you head home? You've had a long night," Bill added.

Nellie paused, glanced at the scorched Crepe home, turned, and walked to her car with the dispersing crowd.

"I'd like your men to check for footprints around the property, particularly near the kitchen window," Colleen said when she and Bill were alone.

"What's on your mind?" Bill asked.

"Arson."

"You think we're dealing with a homicide?"

Colleen nodded. Bill studied her a moment. Colleen knew that look. It meant he thought she was asking him based on a hunch, on her dreaded gut. Oh well. It didn't matter. She'd get the impressions with or without his help.

"Rodney, get the men around the house. Let me know if you find any footprints," Bill called to his deputy and turned back to Colleen. "Anything else?"

Colleen was stunned. He had done what she asked without question. He made it hard for her to stay mad at him when he acted like that. Maybe she should be the one who started the apologies.

"Bill, about this morning," she said, but before she could continue a car rounded the corner and blinded them with its headlights.

Colleen and Bill raised their hands to shield their eyes from the light. The car slowed and stopped before them. The engine and lights still on, they heard the car door open and slam closed. Colleen squinted and tried to make out the driver.

"Hey, cut the lights," Bill said.

A hulking shadow emerged from the dark and waddled into the light.

"Bobby," Colleen said to herself, a sinking feeling in her stomach.

"Mind turning off those lights, Bobby?" Bill asked, gently this time.

Bobby disappeared and the lights went out. He shuffled toward them.

"I'll handle this," Bill said to Colleen and walked to meet Bobby halfway.

Colleen watched Bobby as Bill talked to him about what had happened. In her experience, when people arrived to find their home damaged or destroyed by fire with a loved one having perished inside they were distraught, an expression of anguish on their faces. Colleen found it curious that the younger Crepe seemed oddly calm. But everyone reacted to loss differently, she reminded herself. Perhaps she misread Bobby's reaction. Perhaps his lack of emotion meant he was in shock.

Colleen surveyed her team to see how they were doing with the salvage and overhaul—a critical stage in the firefighting process. A rekindled fire was something to be avoided at all costs. If firefighters had to return to a scene due to a rekindle it often meant the loss of resident lives and firefighter jobs. Her guys were nearing completion and would be able to take-up soon. Movement from the azaleas near Myrtle's house caught her eye. Colleen stared at the bushes and waited. The plants rustled again. Something or someone was in the shrubs.

Colleen cautiously approached the foliage at the edge of the property. The image of the man with the gun at the Currituck Beach Lighthouse flashed through her mind. She hesitated then moved forward, reasoning that nobody would shoot her with so many emergency and law enforcement personnel present. She inched closer to the brush.

"Hello?" she said. Nothing. "Is someone there?" Again nothing. Colleen exhaled and tipped her hat back. She was tired. Her mind was playing tricks on her. It was probably a possum or raccoon. She turned away.

"Burn burn burn," came a voice from behind her.

Colleen whipped around and came face to face with Crazy Charlie. Charlie Nuckels was a large, thick man, the kind who could have been a strongman in the carnivals when they still traveled up the East Coast from Gibbtown, Florida. Unfortunately for Charlie, the community, and vacationers, Charlie had no awareness of his immense size. After Charlie had accidentally jumped on children twice while playing in the sand and once nearly drowned a nine-year-old girl while boogie boarding in the surf, Colleen and Bill had agreed that Charlie needed to be barred from the beach. They hadn't wanted to ban him but it had become unsafe not to. Charlie wasn't so much crazy as mentally different. The local kids had nicknamed him Crazy Charlie decades ago, mostly for the bizarre things he said, and the name had stuck.

"What are you doing here, Charlie?" Colleen asked.

"Burn burn burn," he said, bouncing up and down.

"It's okay. The fire is out. You don't need to worry," she said, trying to reassure him.

"Burn burn burn!" Charlie screamed back at her.

"Shut him up!" shouted Bobby, storming toward her and Charlie. Bobby was no longer calm. He was enraged.

"Burn burn burn!" Charlie squealed again with delight.

Bill reached out to grab Bobby, but Bobby was too quick and waddled toward Charlie at full speed. Colleen stepped in front of Charlie to block him from Bobby's attack. Charlie giggled wildly behind her. She prayed she didn't get sandwiched between the two men before Bill had a chance to pull Bobby away.

Colleen put her arm up to stop the approaching Bobby. As his chest pushed into her palm, Bill got a secure hold on Bobby and yanked him back.

"I want him arrested!" Bobby yelled, pointing at Charlie and attempting to break free of Bill.

"Bobby burn burn burn! Bobby burn burn burn!" Charlie shrieked.

Colleen's men noticed the ruckus and rushed forward to pull Charlie away so he couldn't antagonize Bobby. It took several of them to accomplish the task but eventually they got him a safe distance away. After Colleen made sure Bill still had Bobby, she faced Charlie.

"Quiet now," she said. "You're upsetting Bobby. You don't really want to do that, do you?"

"Yes," Charlie said, grinning and bobbing his head up and down.

"Now, Charlie, you better stop or Sheriff Dorman will have to take you down to the station. You know how much you like the station."

Charlie folded his arms over his broad chest and jutted out his lower lip in a defiant pout.

"I want him arrested," Bobby said, still trying to break free of Bill but with much less energy than before.

"No!" Charlie said and turned his back.

Colleen widened her eyes in disbelief. This was becoming a circus.

"We don't have any reason to take Charlie in," Bill said to Bobby.

"You heard him. He burned my house down! He killed my mother!"

Bill used his strength to gently but firmly move Bobby away. Colleen could hear Bill trying to calm Bobby. "Come on," he said in a low voice, "you know how Charlie can be. He says things that don't mean anything."

"What's he doing here then?" Bobby asked.

It was a good question. Charlie didn't live on this part of Corolla and it wouldn't be the first time he had set something on fire. Several years ago Charlie had accidentally set dune grass on fire with matches he had found in a public garbage bin. Fortunately, a quick-thinking vacationer had doused the fire with a hose before it reached his beach house.

"Bobby has a point," Colleen said to Bill. "This isn't Charlie's neighborhood."

"See, Chief McCabe agrees with me," Bobby said.

Bill frowned at her. Uh-oh. The last thing she needed was Bill thinking she had ganged up on him.

"I didn't say that," she said. "I just don't think it's in Charlie's nature. I mean, look at him."

Charlie was now happily wearing Jimmy's helmet, which teetered several sizes too small on the top of his large round head.

"I'm still going to have to question him," Bill said.

Colleen knew Bill was right. She also knew how upset Charlie would be.

"And you, too, Bobby."

"Me?" Bobby said with a gasp.

"You can't be serious," Colleen said.

Bill glared at her. Oops. Why couldn't she keep her big mouth shut?

"If there's nothing further, I'll go check on my guys," she said and tried not to appear in a hurry as she scurried away. She was glad she had her protective gear on. Bill could have burned a hole in her back with that look.

Colleen approached Jimmy. "Everything okay, Chief?" he asked.

"Bill needs to question Charlie at the station," she said in a whisper. "You up for helping me to get him to go?"

Jimmy gave her a thumbs-up.

"Hey, Charlie," Colleen said. "You mind helping Jimmy and me figure out what happened with the fire?"

"You mean like a junior firefighter?" he asked.

"Sure, like a junior firefighter," she said.

"What do I have to do?"

"Nothing much. Just tell Sheriff Dorman what you saw."

Charlie's shoulders dropped and his eyebrows furrowed. "Do I have to go to the station?"

"Only for a little while. Then you can go home."

Charlie shook his head.

"I bet the sheriff will let you turn on the lights in his car when you're done," Jimmy said.

"Really?" he asked.

"I'll make sure he does," Jimmy said. "How about it, big man?"

Charlie eyed Colleen and Jimmy. She could feel her firefighters holding their breath, waiting. "Come on, Charlie. What do you say?" she said.

Charlie paused then said simply, "Okay."

"Thataboy," Jimmy said. "Let's you and I go tell the sheriff."

Jimmy patted Charlie on the back and took him to Bill, who helped Charlie into his vehicle. Colleen searched the area for Bobby and spotted him sitting in his car, watching. She was relieved that Bill had decided to question Bobby later. Losing a family member and your home was traumatic. He didn't need to be put through an interrogation, at least not tonight.

For the second time that evening, Colleen was blinded by approaching headlights. This time she recognized the vehicle. It was the coroner's. The SUV slowed and stopped in front of the house. Bill met the coroner as he exited his vehicle. After a brief exchange, they continued toward the house. Bobby hopped from his car and hurried after them.

"Bobby," Colleen called and sprinted to intercept him.

"I want to see her," Bobby said.

"I don't think that's a good idea."

"I didn't know she was . . . why was she . . ." Bobby choked out before breaking down in tears.

Colleen was sorry she had questioned Bobby's earlier reaction. He was clearly grieving. They all were. She patted his back and found herself in a sudden bear hug. Bobby's sobs increased in volume. She braced herself against his weight as he crumpled in her arms.

"I know," she said, awkwardly tapping his back. Colleen felt her eyes welling with tears. It wasn't fair. Myrtle may have been a nuisance, but it was part of what gave her her spunk. She still had a lot of life in her. How dare someone do this to her.

Colleen caught sight of the coroner's team making their way from the house with Myrtle's body. Bobby saw the body bag and broke down sobbing again. Bill's eyes widened in surprise. Colleen signaled him that she had things under control and watched over Bobby's shoulder as his mother's body was quietly, somberly lifted into the coroner's SUV and taken away.

"Do you have someone you can stay with?" she asked Bobby after the vehicle had been gone a moment.

"Yeah," he said through sniffles, released her, and backed away. "Sorry."

"You have nothing to be sorry about."

He shrugged, shuffled back to his car, squeezed in, and drove off.

Bill pulled out next with Charlie in the back seat. She gave them a short wave, then ordered her squad back to the station. The men removed the wheel stops, slipped out of their coats, and took their seats inside the engine. Colleen allowed the engine to leave ahead of her, gave the Crepe residence a final once-over, and drove out of the neighborhood.

As Colleen made her way back to the firehouse, exhaustion set in. She loosened her ponytail and rolled down the window. Maybe the fresh air would revive her. She stole a glance at Sparky asleep on the front seat. The dog half opened his eyes and closed them again. Colleen wished she could head straight home to her soft, cool bed, but she needed to speak to the men about what had happened before they showered and hit the bunks.

Despite the loss of life, she was pleased by how her team had performed. They had worked safely and efficiently. There was nothing more they could have done to save Myrtle. Most important, nobody got hurt. Since she had become chief, not a single man in her company had suffered a serious injury. It was a record she was proud of and wanted to keep. Every firefighter knew that putting his or her life in danger meant putting the entire team in danger. Colleen pulled into the driveway behind the engine. Sparky moaned to be let out. She opened the door, slid out, and called for him so he could take care of business before they went home later.

When Colleen entered the community room, she found the men already in mid-undress. They were used to her seeing them in their boxer briefs and T-shirts, even if she wasn't. The worst time had been when one of the guys had had a new tattoo of the Whalehead Fire and Rescue shield inked under his belly button. Everyone had reacted except her. When the men had asked her what she thought, she had acted nonchalant and gave it her seal of approval. To display discomfort would have highlighted that she was a woman in a man's world. She had worked too hard to break down barriers and create a close, family atmosphere. She wasn't going to let a silly thing like her uneasiness at seeing her men half-naked ruin that.

Colleen was acutely aware of how she, as a woman, had disrupted the station when she came on board. The common showers, changing area, bathroom, and sleeping quarters weren't going to work anymore, especially if they were going to bring on women firefighters. In preparation for hiring women, she had had plans drawn up to have the station renovated with separate shower, dressing, and bathroom facilities. She and the men had decided as a group that there was no need for separate sleeping quarters. Those would continue to be reserved according to status, not gender. The renovations were scheduled to begin in the fall when their call load lightened and the weather cooled.

"Everyone's here, Chief," Jimmy said while yanking a clean T-shirt over his head.

Colleen began her debriefing. She kept it short, knowing the men were tired and that they'd have a longer meeting the next day. They started with thoughts and prayers for Myrtle. Some even joked about how they would miss her cranky remarks. Colleen praised the team for their dedication and selflessness, reminded them to check their gear and to let Jimmy know if they discovered any problems, and then ordered them to get some sleep.

As the firefighters headed to the showers, Colleen dragged herself up the stairs to her office to change out of her gear. She couldn't wait until the station renovations were under way. The screen she had put up in her office corner to change behind just wasn't cutting it. It reminded her too much of the changing area at her gynecologist's office.

After slipping into jeans and a T-shirt, Colleen spent time completing paperwork while the details of the call were fresh in her mind. By the time she finished, the station had fallen quiet. She wearily turned off her desk light and plodded downstairs. She waved at a couple of the men who were watching television in the recreation room as she passed. They sleepily acknowledged her, then returned to the television. She called for Sparky, who instantly appeared from a dark corner of the garage. Finally, it was time to go home.

Chapter 5

Colleen yawned as she pulled into her driveway. As the SUV slowed to a stop, Sparky lifted himself and blinked sleepily. Colleen cut the engine and lights and allowed the blanket of night to envelop her. She listened to the water lapping at her bayside pier, a toad croaking an intermittent melody, and a bat fluttering overhead catching insects. She loved how peaceful and quiet the world became late at night. She felt her eyelids grow heavy and realized she was in danger of falling asleep in her car. Colleen opened the driver's-side door and slid from the seat. Sparky clumsily jumped out behind her. She rubbed her neck and stretched her arms, relieved to finally be home.

Colleen dragged herself up the front porch steps and put the key into the lock. She was surprised that Sparky didn't rush by her in his usual eagerness to be first in. She walked to the edge of the porch and spotted his white muzzle in the shadows. He was staring at a group of azalea bushes that bordered the path that led to the back of the house. His head was cocked slightly to the side with one ear up.

"Not now, fella. It's late." That's all she needed—Sparky chasing after a raccoon in the middle of the night. "Heel," she said with more force.

She was relieved when Sparky obediently bounced toward her. He wasn't always so easy to get in. The dog paused to steal a look back, then lumbered into the dark house. A loud hiss came from within. Colleen flipped on the foyer light in time to see Smokey, her cranky twelve-year-old Siamese, take a swipe at Sparky's backside as he trotted toward his dog bed in the living room.

"Leave him alone, sourpuss," she said to the cat as she closed the front door.

Smokey let out an angry howl. Colleen slipped out of her shoes and padded into the kitchen. There would be no sleep until Smokey was fed; the cat would see to that. Smokey rubbed against her legs as she cracked open a can of Fancy Feast Ocean Whitefish and Tuna. It was the only brand and flavor Smokey would eat. Colleen scraped the food onto a saucer, gave it to Smokey, and joined the cat on the floor. The clicking of Sparky's nails warned Colleen that he was coming to steal Smokey's food. As the Border collie rounded the corner, she put her leg up against the wall to block him. The dog heaved a sigh and flopped down beside her. He'd wait until the finicky feline was done.

Colleen surveyed her combined kitchen and dining room. It was cheerful, comfortable, and for the most part neat. The décor was part Southern charm, part Petsmart clearance. Her mother had helped her with the Southern charm: cheerful white cotton curtains with a blue starfish print; cherrywood furniture with clean simple lines; and oil paintings and watercolors of the island by local artists. Sparky had helped with the PetSmart clearance: squeaky rubber toys of bones and cats; several partially chewed pigs' ears; and a padded window seat for Smokey that the cat had yet to use.

Colleen remembered when she had found this place. It had been advertised as a fisherman's delight, primarily because it was located on a remote part of the northern sound side of the island. When the sales agent had opened the door, the overpowering smell of fish had made Colleen wonder if anyone, even a fisherman, could find the house delightful. The residence had clearly been used as a flophouse for sportsmen and came "as is." Still, beneath the dirt and disrepair, Colleen had seen potential. The realtor had told her that it may be too much of a challenge for Colleen to fix it up with Colleen being a single woman and all. That had gotten her Irish dander up and she had made an offer on the spot. With some help from friends who worked as contractors, she had transformed the rundown dwelling into a place she called home.

As Smokey was finishing the last of her meal, Sparky growled, causing the cat to quickly scurry off. "Hey," Colleen said, scolding the dog. But it wasn't the food that had his attention. Sparky ran to the foyer and barked at the front door. Someone was outside her house. In an instant, adrenaline surged through Colleen's body. What if it was the man with the gun? What if he was there to hurt her or set fire to her house?

Colleen quickly crawled to the hall closet and grabbed a hammer from the toolbox on the floor. She clicked the lights off, leapt to the front door, and listened. The floorboards on the porch steps creaked under the weight of the intruder. Colleen carefully wrapped her fingers around the doorknob. If the man tried to come in he was going to get a hammer to the head. She hefted the hammer in her right hand to make sure she had it balanced for maximum force. The footsteps drew closer, shuffled to the front door, and stopped. She raised the hammer. Sparky growled. Colleen gave him a quick shush. Sparky sat back on his haunches and all went silent.

Colleen felt her heart pounding in her chest. She squeezed the hammer, the muscles in her forearm and biceps tightening. She held her breath. The clock on the mantel in the living room ticked quietly. Colleen felt her intruder's presence on the other side of the door. What was he doing out there? She pressed her ear to the door to see if she could hear what he was up to.

Bang! Bang! Bang!

Colleen jerked back. "Colleen McCabe, open this door!"

Colleen threw the porch light switch on and yanked open the door, the hammer still raised in her right hand. Standing before her, hair wildly askew, face filthy, clothes in disarray and slightly singed, was Myrtle Crepe. To Colleen, Myrtle looked like a troll doll she had had as a child. The two women stood, frozen for a second, staring at one another.

"You're alive!" Colleen finally said with genuine enthusiasm, lowered the hammer, and seized Myrtle in a hug.

"For heaven's sake, let me go!" Myrtle screamed.

Colleen released Myrtle. "I thought you were dead."

"Aren't you going to let me in?!" Myrtle screamed again.

"You don't have to yell."

Myrtle squinted at Colleen and tilted an ear toward her. "What? Speak up!"

Colleen suddenly realized what was going on. Myrtle had been near her home when it exploded. No wonder she was shouting. She was having trouble hearing.

"Why don't you come in?" Colleen said.

"What?!"

"Come in!" Colleen said, raising her voice, and motioned for Myrtle to enter.

"It's about time!" Myrtle yelled and stepped inside.

Colleen surveyed her yard, still concerned about an intruder, then closed the front door and locked it. She walked toward the kitchen and signaled Myrtle to follow. Sparky trailed Myrtle, sniffing her smoky clothes as he went. Colleen removed a glass from a cabinet and held it near the filtered-water dispenser on the refrigerator door to indicate to Myrtle she was offering a glass of water.

"Thank you!" Myrtle said, still speaking loudly.

Colleen filled the glass, handed it to Myrtle, and studied her as she guzzled the water. Myrtle's hand was shaking and she needed medical attention, but the bottom line was Myrtle was alive. Relief washed over Colleen with every gulp Myrtle took. She hadn't sent her former teacher to her death! But then who had the coroner taken away? Myrtle finished the water and handed Colleen the glass.

"Another?" Colleen asked.

"You trying to drown me?"

Colleen couldn't help but smile. The explosion hadn't knocked Myrtle's sass out of her. She put the glass in the sink. "Come on," she said, motioning Myrtle out of the room.

She led Myrtle into the living room and gestured for her to sit in a high-back chair. Colleen sat on a nearby ottoman as Myrtle tried to tame her wild hair.

"You need to go to the hospital."

"I'm fine," Myrtle said, this time at a more normal volume.

Good, Colleen thought, Myrtle's hearing was coming back. "I'm calling the station. Just to be sure," she said, moving toward the phone.

Myrtle clutched Colleen's arm and held on tight. Colleen turned back, surprised. She could have easily broken Myrtle's grip but it was the pleading look in Myrtle's eyes that stopped her from pulling away and reaching for the phone. She sat on the ottoman and Myrtle released her.

"Myrtle," she said, this time more gently, "you need someone to check you out."

"Then you do it."

Colleen sighed. Very well. She got up, retrieved a medical kit from the closet in the kitchen, rolled the ottoman closer to Myrtle, opened the case, and removed a stethoscope and blood pressure cuff. She held out the cuff but hesitated in midair. Other than grabbing Myrtle's arm when the man with the gun had appeared earlier this evening, she had never touched her teacher before. Touching Myrtle was somehow like touching a nun. It just wasn't done.

"What's wrong?" Myrtle asked, worry creeping over her face.

Time to be professional. She didn't want to cause Myrtle unnecessary alarm. She took Myrtle's arm and wrapped the cuff around it. She was surprised by how soft Myrtle's skin was. It was nothing like the tough exterior she projected.

"What day is it?" Colleen asked.

Myrtle rolled her eyes. "For Pete's sake. July fourth. My name is Myrtle Mae Crepe. I am of sound mind. And someone tried to kill me!"

Okay. She would skip the orientation questions. Myrtle was clearly lucid; she didn't want to make her livid, too. Getting Myrtle angry wouldn't help her blood pressure. The room fell silent as Colleen finished taking the reading. She couldn't believe it. The woman had survived an explosion and her blood pressure was 115 over 80. "Your blood pressure's normal."

"I told you I'm fine. Now can we stop this foolishness? We've got a murderer running loose."

"How do you know about that?" Colleen asked, surprised.

"What do you mean, how do I know? When I was walking to my back door my house exploded. Why I listened to you, I'll never know. If I had just stayed—"

"No," Colleen said, interrupting. "I mean, how did you know about the body?"

"Body? What body?" Myrtle asked, puzzled.

"The one that was found in your house."

"There was a body in my house?" Myrtle said, her voice squeaking. Then her eyes widened. "Bobby!"

"Bobby's fine," Colleen said. "He thinks you're dead. But otherwise he's fine."

"Then who was in my house?"

"That's what I was hoping you could tell me. Start at the beginning. What exactly happened?" Colleen put her medical equipment away. Her long night was getting longer.

"Someone was in my house, before it exploded. I think a man."

"The man we saw earlier at the Lighthouse?"

"I don't know. I didn't have my glasses on."

"I thought you said you didn't wear glasses."

Myrtle pursed her lips, caught in a lie.

A slight smile formed at the edges of Colleen's lips. So Myrtle had a vain streak. "You said you saw someone?"

Myrtle shrugged. "Not exactly. No. It was more of a gut feeling, you know?"

Yeah, Colleen thought, I know. "Does anyone else know you're alive?"

"No. And we're going to keep it that way," Myrtle said with finality.

"We have to notify people that you're okay."

"If we tell people I'm alive, whoever tried to kill me will try again."

"We don't know if you were targeted, Myrtle."

"It was *my* house. Who else would they be after? What happened to that person . . . it was meant for me."

"Speaking of that other person," Colleen began, "it was a woman. Someone you hired, perhaps? Maybe a maid?"

"What? And let someone ruin my organization system?"

Colleen resisted the urge to tell Myrtle what she thought of her "system." "Maybe a friend of Bobby's, then?"

"Please," Myrtle said with a dismissive wave. "Bobby knows better than to have a woman in my house."

"Okay," Colleen said, not really wanting to get into Bobby's dating life. "Can you think of anybody, besides the man with the gun, who might have broken in to hurt you?"

"Who would want to hurt me?" Myrtle asked, genuinely stumped.

"Oh, I don't know . . . belittled students, tortured colleagues, humiliated waitstaff . . . anyone in Corolla."

"All right, all right. I get the point. So I've ruffled a few feathers."

That's one way of putting it, Colleen thought. "So you don't know who was in your house or why?"

"No," Myrtle said, discouraged. "But the murderer must have thought it was me. And if he finds out it wasn't, I won't be safe."

Colleen hated to admit it but Myrtle had a point. She wasn't sure if the sheriff's department could protect Myrtle from what might be a professional hitman. "But what about Bobby?"

she asked. Myrtle wouldn't really want her son to worry. Would she?

"Little Bobby will understand our need for secrecy after you and I have caught these criminals."

"Hold on. Since when did we become Nancy Drew and Miss Marple?"

"Since I walked my old bones all the way here in the middle of the night. Besides, you saw the gangster with the gun. Your life could be in danger, too."

Colleen got up and paced the room. Her earlier joy at seeing Myrtle had changed to exasperation. What Myrtle was asking her to do was crazy. She could easily investigate the arson, maybe even do some digging behind Bill's back, but concealing Myrtle's status as one of the living from the coroner, and from Bill, was pushing things too far. Bill would kill her if he found out—that is, if the men responsible for blowing up Myrtle's house didn't get to her first. She cracked her knuckles.

"Well?" Myrtle asked from the high-back chair.

Colleen took a deep breath. "Look, Myrtle, I—"

Sparky suddenly growled at the front door. Colleen peeked through the front curtains. Headlights swung into her driveway and a vehicle with the sheriff's department seal stopped in front of the house. "Crap," she said.

"What is it?" Myrtle asked.

Colleen grabbed her firefighter baseball cap from the sofa and pulled it tight over Myrtle's head. "Stay low and don't say a word."

Bill's approaching footsteps made Sparky growl again. The knock on the door made him bark. Colleen approached the door.

She stole a look back at Myrtle. She could just see the top of the baseball cap. Another knock. Colleen paused a moment before opening the door a crack. "Bill, what are you doing here?" she asked, blocking his view of the living room.

Bill twirled his hat in his hands. She waited. Their eyes locked. Her heart raced with nervousness. "How are you?" he asked.

"Fine," she said.

Bill cleared his throat. "I'm sorry. I know this must be tough . . . how important it is to you that you save . . ." He took a deep breath and began again. "I'm sure Myrtle was gone before you arrived. You did everything you could."

"Yes, well . . ." Colleen said, trying to think of a reasonable response, given that she knew Myrtle was alive and well and sitting a few feet away in her living room.

"I could stay. We can talk if you'd like."

"No!" Colleen said, panicked.

Bill raised his head in surprise.

"I mean," she said, trying to cover, "that's really not necessary. But nice of you to offer."

She studied Bill. His uniform was slightly wrinkled; his brown eyes were tired. Colleen thought he was especially handsome in the soft glow of the porch light. This was the shy, vulnerable side of Bill that people rarely saw. It was the side that made her wonder if they would ever become more than professional colleagues. The sound of something dropping on the floor of her living room snapped Colleen back to the present moment.

"Yes, well, it's been a long night. Thank you for coming by," she said.

Bill attempted to see into the house but Colleen blocked the opening. "Are you sure you're okay?" he asked, now on full alert.

"Of course. I'm tired, that's all."

Suddenly, Myrtle started coughing, loud and deep. Bill's brows raised in surprise, then furrowed in hurt anger.

"I didn't realize you had company," he said, an edge to his voice.

Colleen forced a weak smile as Myrtle coughed and cleared her throat behind her. Bill put on his hat and turned away.

"Good night," Colleen said, unable to think of anything else.

"Good night" was Bill's curt response as he stormed down the steps.

Colleen closed and gently locked the door. As soon as she heard the engine start on Bill's SUV, she marched into the living room. "You call that being quiet?" she asked, trying not to lose her temper.

"You were taking so long . . . I needed something to do," Myrtle said, retrieving a gardening book from the floor. "When I bent to get this I started coughing. I was in an explosion, in case you forgot."

Colleen snatched the book from Myrtle. Her head was swimming. She paced the room. What was she going to do now? Bill thought Myrtle was dead and that Colleen had a man over. What if she needed his help later? He might not give it to her if he was angry or jealous.

"So it's official. I'm dead," Myrtle said.

"No, you're not," Colleen said, refocusing on Myrtle. "And I'm telling Bill."

"No, you won't."

"Watch me," Colleen said, grabbed the phone from the end table, and dialed.

"If you had wanted Sheriff Dorman to know, you would have told him when he was here. Admit it. You want to catch the criminals as much as I do."

Colleen clicked the phone off and tossed it on the sofa. Sparky and Myrtle kept an eye on Colleen as she walked back and forth trying to figure out what to do next. Why hadn't she told Bill that Myrtle was here? Was Myrtle right? Did she think she could catch whoever had tried to blow Myrtle up? Was Bill right? Did she stick her nose where it didn't belong? What if it was discovered that she was concealing Myrtle and information critical to the case? Her whole career could be in jeopardy, not to mention her relationship with Bill. Then again, if she managed to solve the real murder and do it while keeping Myrtle safe, no matter how mad Bill got he'd have to see that she'd been helpful, that she had done the right thing, and that she had protected a life, even one as annoying as Myrtle Crepe's. Yes, he would finally see how valuable she was to him.

"So?" Myrtle asked. "What's our plan?"

"There is no plan," Colleen said with a sigh. She plopped down on the sofa, at a loss as to how to proceed.

"We've got to have a plan," Myrtle said. "The killer's still out there."

"I know that," she said, struggling to keep her cool. "I'll see what I can dig up through the arson investigation, but if things get too crazy I'm going to Bill. Until I decide what to do with you, you're staying here. That means no going out, no using the phone, no answering the door, and definitely no snooping."

"You expect me to stay locked up here and do nothing?"

"As long as the killer thinks you're dead he won't come after you again. Staying hidden is the only way you'll be safe."

"What about that body? What happens when they figure out it's not me?"

"They're a little busy in the medical examiner's office right now. Because everyone thinks it's your body, there's no reason to rush to identify it. That buys me time to find out who was after you and murdered that unfortunate person instead."

"But why was she in my house?" Myrtle asked.

"If I knew who she was I might have a better idea," Colleen said. "I imagine her family will report her missing at some point and get confirmation from the coroner. Once that happens, though, you'll be in danger again."

"Which means I have to stay here," Myrtle said, resigned.

"Exactly," she said, glad that Myrtle was finally cooperating. "I'll get clothes from your house for you when I pick up the Preservation Society papers for Nellie."

"But the Society materials are mine!" Myrtle said, leaping up in a huff.

"Fine. I'll just tell Nellie she can't have them *because you're still alive!*"

That shut Myrtle up. She flumped back into the chair, folded her arms, and pouted. Silence fell over the room. Colleen ran her fingers through her hair. Myrtle was so damn aggravating. She could see why someone might want to kill her. A sly smile crept over Myrtle's face and she began giggling to herself. Wonderful, Colleen thought. Myrtle was cracking up. Now she might have to admit a presumably dead woman to the psychiatric ward. "What's so funny?" she asked.

"The sheriff thinks you were with a man," Myrtle said between snickers.

"So?"

"You? Please," Myrtle said with a snort.

Colleen rolled her eyes. Really, Myrtle could be so childish. It was time to put the child to bed. "We should get you settled," Colleen said. "There's a bathroom with a shower down the hall so you can clean up. I'll leave clean sweats outside the door for you. The sofa folds out. You can sleep in the living room."

Myrtle rose and proceeded to the bathroom without a word. Colleen watched her go, surprised at her sudden obedience.

While Myrtle showered, Colleen pulled out the sofa bed and made it up with clean sheets, a fresh cotton blanket, and a fluffed down pillow. Smokey appeared from wherever she had been hiding and jumped on the bed. Colleen shooed the cat, not knowing if Myrtle was allergic or not. Smokey responded with an angry hiss and scurried under the sofa. Sparky put his chin on the blanket and sniffed the sheets.

"Great, not you, too," Colleen said.

Unlike the Siamese, Sparky removed his head from the bed without a fuss and curled up on his dog bed in the corner. Colleen dimmed the lights to a soft, relaxing glow. Myrtle deserved a good night's sleep after what she'd been through, if she could get one.

"That looks nice," Myrtle said.

Colleen found Myrtle standing in the doorway, hair wet, and dressed in the sweatpants Colleen had placed outside the bathroom door. "How do you feel?" she asked.

"Tired," Myrtle said. "Whose pants are these?"

"My father's. He left them here the last time he visited. It's all I had that"—Colleen stopped herself before finishing the sentence—"would fit you."

"They'll do," Myrtle said, padded to the sofa bed, and slid under the sheets.

"I'll let you get some sleep," she said and turned to go.

"Colleen?"

Colleen paused. "Yes?"

"Would you mind staying, at least until I fall asleep?"

Colleen looked at Myrtle tucked into the bed like a little girl.

"Please," Myrtle said, eyes welling with tears. The events of the night were sinking in.

Colleen's protective instincts kicked in. "Of course," she said.

Smokey reemerged, jumped on the bed, and curled up next to Myrtle. "Smokey, no," Colleen ordered, ready to pluck the cat from the bed and lock her in the mudroom.

"It's okay," Myrtle said and rubbed the cat's cheek. "I like cats."

Colleen heard Smokey purr from across the room. She shook her head. Figures, the one person the cranky cat took to was the cranky schoolteacher. Colleen scooped a magazine from the coffee table and settled into a chair where she could keep an eye on Myrtle and the front door. She flipped through the pages, searching for an article she had been meaning to finish.

"Good night, Colleen," Myrtle said, her voice already heavy with sleep.

Myrtle's breathing became slow and steady. Colleen rose and quietly crossed to the foyer. "Good night, Myrtle," she said in a whisper and switched off the light.

Chapter 6

The news of Myrtle Crepe's death spread quickly through the Outer Banks. Currituck County was no stranger to its share of trouble but such troubles consisted mostly of drunk driving arrests, domestic disturbances, and theft of construction materials—not murder. Colleen spent the next week fielding questions from reporters about the arson investigation, fighting with Myrtle about her need to stay hidden at the house, and painfully coping with Bill's distant, all-business attitude. With neither work nor home offering relief from the tension, Colleen was growing increasingly irritable and the guys at the station were bearing the brunt of it.

To make matters worse, today was Myrtle's memorial service. Little Bobby had made arrangements despite the lack of a coroner's report. The medical examiner's office was backlogged and, since no one had reported a woman missing, it didn't seem likely they would have a final report for weeks. Bobby had no reason to believe that the body was anyone other than his mother and didn't see the point in waiting.

Colleen was sick to her stomach as she drove to the Corolla Chapel to pay her respects. She hated attending the service of someone she knew wasn't really dead. It felt like bad karma. All week she had racked her brain trying to come up with a legitimate excuse for why she couldn't be at Myrtle's memorial ceremony, but she recognized that her absence would raise eyebrows. Everyone in Corolla who had loved *or* hated Myrtle would be there.

It was the prospect of observing and identifying potential suspects that kept Colleen driving to the chapel located a few blocks north of the Currituck Beach Lighthouse. Perhaps the killer would come to the service to admire his or her handiwork. Or better yet, maybe she would get lucky and the killer would feel a need to confess to the crime before the congregation. She understood a confession was highly unlikely, so she'd fall back on observing everyone in attendance—even those least likely to commit such a horrible crime. The sooner she figured out who the guilty party was, the sooner she could get her life back.

Earlier, Myrtle had begged to go with her to witness the memorial service, even clutching Colleen around the waist and refusing to let go as Colleen tried to leave. Myrtle had promised Colleen she would remain hidden in the SUV under a blanket. She only wanted to see how many people showed, how much people missed her. In some bizarre way, she had understood Myrtle's curiosity. Who wouldn't want to see what type of impact they had made on the world? It was only by promising Myrtle a blow-by-blow account of the service that Colleen had been able to get her to remain at the house. Colleen hoped someone had something nice to say about Myrtle. Otherwise, she'd have to make something up. She could certainly concoct a few nice words but, given her general irritation with her house guest, Colleen wasn't sure she'd be that convincing.

As she pulled into the parking lot of the Corolla Chapel, a lump formed in her throat at the sight of Bill's SUV. She made a point of parking in a space on the opposite side of the lot. She cut the engine and let out a heavy sigh. In the last week Bill had been aloof, speaking to her only when it concerned the case. Part of Bill's behavior had to do with his being busy with the homicide investigation and press conferences; the rest had to do with Bill thinking she had a male companion. If he only knew the "companion" he thought he had heard the night of the explosion was anything but.

The sound of a motorcycle revving in the parking lot put an end to Colleen's ruminations. She turned to see who would be rude enough to make such a racket at a memorial service and was surprised to discover Little Bobby Crepe atop a shiny new Harley. Bobby wobbled into a space, sputtered to a stop, and attempted to heave his chubby leg over the seat. The dismount was made all the more difficult because of the stiff black leather chaps he was wearing. He eventually managed to maneuver his leg over the top and teetered as he regained his balance. Colleen noted his new boots, blue jeans, black leather jacket, and helmet and watched him stand back to admire his new bike gleaming in the bright July sun. He gently brushed a speck of dust from its seat, then headed into the church. She couldn't help but notice there was now a slight swagger to his waddle.

Colleen sat in her vehicle, stunned. Little Bobby, uniformed preservation officer, was now Big Bobby, leather-wearing biker. As the shock wore off, she wondered how she was going to tell Myrtle about this. And then it struck her: this was certainly an odd way for a grieving son to behave, especially at his mother's memorial service. At least he's wearing black, she thought. She recalled Bobby's reaction the night of the explosion. Had she mistaken guilt for grief? As improbable as it seemed, Bobby Crepe became her first suspect.

Colleen exited her SUV and instantly wished she weren't in dress uniform. The temperature was already in the mid-eighties and it was only mid-morning. She tugged uncomfortably at her jacket, partially to keep it from sticking to her skin and partially because she hated memorials and funerals. She found it incredibly difficult to witness the loss felt by those left behind and usually found her eyes welling with tears even if she didn't know the deceased. She was not in danger of weeping today, however, since Myrtle wasn't really dead. Instead, she'd feel like a heel watching everyone go through emotional heartbreak. As distasteful as the deception was, it was necessary in order to protect Myrtle.

She advanced toward the front door of the chapel and admired how cheerful the chapel's white paint appeared in the morning sun. The original one-room Corolla Chapel had been built in 1885 by two carpenters after the local community had formed a congregation. For the next seventy-three years the chapel had been on a Baptist circuit or had visiting pastors. Eventually, the chapel fell into disuse and it wasn't until 1988 that a pastor and his wife, John and Ruth Strauss, were convinced by parishioners to start year-round services. In 2002, due to the growth of the congregation and the desire to add to the building, the original chapel was moved across the street to its current location and attached to the new wing. As far as Colleen was concerned, the chapel was a must-see for anyone visiting Corolla.

Colleen entered the cool interior of the church and was instantly greeted by Richard Bailey, the oldest son of Bailey and Sons Funeral Services. "How's it going, Rich?" she asked, taking a program.

"Got a pretty decent turnout. Reporter's here," he said, indicating a handsome young man standing in the right rear corner whispering to a bearded cameraman. "Bill's on the other side," he said and pointed to the left rear corner.

Great, Colleen thought, trapped between the press and Bill. She forced a smile and headed toward the second pew from the back near the aisle.

She quickly took a seat, hoping not to draw Bill's or the reporter's attention. One would want to flee from her, the other run toward her—and it wouldn't be the way she wanted. The choir director played the piano at the front of the chapel as people trickled in. Colleen had always liked the intimacy of the chapel and especially admired the stained-glass window near the altar. She found it entirely fitting that the window of an island chapel depicted images of a flame, a pelican, and an anchor.

Colleen surveyed the room. Rich was right; it was a decent crowd. She recognized the local islanders, many of whom were former students, and nodded to a few as their eyes met. Myrtle's former teaching colleagues were evident by their dress: dark floral skirts, sensible shoes, cardigans even in the middle of summer, and chains around their necks for their bifocals. Scattered among the locals and former colleagues were a handful of curious vacationers. Not anticipating attending a funeral while on holiday, the tourists wore colorful summer attire over their pink sunburned skin. Colleen liked the bit of color they added to the scene.

She spotted Bobby in the front pew sitting near an enormous picture of Myrtle displayed on an easel. She couldn't help but grin at the photo of Myrtle proudly dressed in her Lighthouse Wild Horse Preservation Society uniform and sternly staring back at them. This was no airbrushed photograph for a school yearbook. This was a photo of Myrtle to her stubborn, exasperating core. Colleen could already hear Myrtle snorting her approval when Colleen told her later today. The music stopped and Pastor Fred took the pulpit.

"Ladies and gentlemen, we are gathered here today in memory of our dearly departed Myrtle Mae Crepe. I'd like to start with something I found in a Hallmark card that I thought was appropriate."

Colleen rolled her eyes. A Hallmark card? Certainly the Good Book had words appropriate for the occasion. Well, she thought, he wasn't called Flaky Fred for nothing. As Fred commenced his greeting-card eulogy, Colleen noticed Nellie lean toward Bobby in the front pew and pat his back. Based on Bobby's behavior in the parking lot Colleen wondered if he needed any comforting.

Colleen felt a presence loom over her and discovered Pinky Salvatore standing in the aisle. "May I?" he asked, motioning to the space next to her. Colleen slid over. Normally she'd cringe at the thought of having to sit through anything, memorial service or otherwise, next to Pinky but today was different. She had promised herself that if she ran into Pinky she'd be polite, maybe even charming, in an effort to get information about his whereabouts on the night of July fourth.

Despite being in an interdenominational church, Pinky knelt and genuflected in Catholic tradition before sliding into the pew. Colleen forced a sideways smile at Pinky. Pinky smiled a perfectly white, minty-fresh smile back. Out of the corner of her eye, Colleen caught Bill observing her in jealous disapproval and her smile quickly faded. She faced forward and pulled her arms in tight so as not to have physical contact with her pewmate.

"It's unfortunate what happened to Mrs. Crepe," Pinky said after an awkward silence.

"Yes," Colleen said casually but her mind was racing. Here was her opportunity to interrogate Pinky. Even if he was Myrtle's killer and got angry at her, what could he do? He certainly wouldn't attack her in church. "I've been wondering, Mr. Salvatore . . ." she said.

"Please, call me Pinky."

"Okay, Pinky, what exactly is your association with the fireworks company that came to Corolla last week?"

"It's public knowledge I'm friends with the owner of the company," Pinky said matter-of-factly.

"It seems an interesting coincidence that we have a company

experienced in explosives in town the same night Myrtle's house went up in flames," she said, trying to maintain a casual tone.

"And what, might I ask, does one have to do with the other?"

"It's no secret you and Myrtle didn't get along."

"With all due respect to the departed, Mrs. Crepe failed to get along with a lot of people," Pinky said, surveying the activity at the front of the church.

He has a point, Colleen thought. "Yes, but you're the only one with friends that make things go boom."

"Certainly you don't think I had anything to do with her demise," Pinky said, amused.

"Did you?" she asked.

Pinky slid his arm along the back of the pew behind her. Colleen forced herself not to move. His cologne filled her nostrils and she was surprised to discover that it smelled nice. She had to hand it to Pinky, he had good taste. She could see how some women might find him interesting, but she wasn't one of them.

"Chief McCabe, let me assure you. I'm a legitimate real estate developer. I have no interest in acquiring property through illegal means. It only complicates the process."

"I'm not asking how you acquire property; I'm asking about your friends from New Jersey. Perhaps there's someone with the company who might do you a favor?"

Pinky withdrew his arm. "And we were getting on so nicely."

"Well?" Colleen said, panicking that her opportunity to question Pinky was slipping away.

"If you wish to continue this discussion, come by my trailer.

Now, if you'll excuse me," Pinky said abruptly, slid from the pew, and disappeared out the back of the chapel.

Damn. She had pushed too hard. Why couldn't she have been more subtle, more charming? What was it her mother always said . . . you can catch more bees with honey? Now she'd have to see Pinky on his turf, not a situation she relished.

As Colleen scanned the crowd for new suspects, a man sitting across the aisle at the far end of a pew several rows ahead of her caught her eye. Her pulse quickened. It was the man she had seen at the fireworks, the attractive one in the orange vest. What was he still doing in Corolla? The company had left town with its crew a week ago. He must have sensed she was staring at him because he peered over his shoulder in her direction. Colleen ducked behind the person in front of her and was relieved when he didn't seem to notice her. Why do I care if he sees me? she wondered, and chastised herself for acting like a thirteen-year-old with a crush. Still, she kept her head down as he slipped from the pew and sauntered past her out the back of the chapel.

It took Colleen a second to collect herself. She left the pew and rushed toward the door. She needed to find out what this man was still doing on the island. She continued toward the vestibule and made eye contact with Bill. He instantly knew something was up and followed her.

Colleen rushed from the building and into the parking lot as the back door to a black limousine was closing. She jogged toward the vehicle as it pulled away and onto Corolla Village Road. She stopped, shielded her eyes from the sun, and watched the car disappear.

"What's up?" Bill asked, joining her.

She studied Bill's face and could see he was concerned, and not just on a professional level. She wanted to tell him what was going on. She hated keeping things from him. But she didn't have enough information yet to keep him from being furious at her when he found out she had been playing detective. "It's nothing," she said and looked away. It was at times like this she wished she could twitch her nose like Samantha in the television show *Bewitched* and disappear.

"Please, look at me," Bill said.

Colleen squinted up at Bill. *Uh-oh, here it comes*. The moment she had been avoiding all week. The moment she had been dreading. The moment Bill confronted her about "the other man." "You don't have to say anything," she said, trying to stop him before he started.

"I'm sorry about the other night. I shouldn't have come to your house without calling. I didn't know you had—"

"I don't have—"

"But I heard—"

"It's not what you think."

"It's okay. I get it. It's just that . . ."

Bill ran his hands through his hair. His jaw clenched. She felt her face flush and the tips of her ears burn and knew it wasn't from the soaring heat index. Was Bill going to say what she hoped he was? The wait was killing her but for once in her life she kept her mouth shut. "Colleen," he said after a long pause, "I know we've never talked about it . . . but I thought at some point you and—"

A primal scream suddenly erupted from the chapel and drowned out Bill's final words. Bill and Colleen stared at each other in stunned silence as if jolted from a deep sleep. When a second scream came they took off running toward the church. Colleen's heart raced as they sprinted across the lot. What if the killer had struck again? A bansheelike cry echoed in the chapel as Bill whipped open the front door. They rushed into the vestibule.

"Thank God you two are here," Rich Bailey said. "I don't know what got into him."

Colleen and Bill hurried into the chapel and discovered Crazy Charlie screaming and doing a jig at the pulpit. "Burn burn burn!" he shrieked and skipped around the stage while waving his arms wildly in the air.

"Come on down from there, Charlie," Pastor Fred said in a soothing voice, attempting to coax Charlie from the pulpit.

"Burn burn burn!" Charlie screeched again, threw his head back, and let out another primal scream.

"How dare you!" Little Bobby yelled from the front pew and charged.

Colleen and Bill ran down the center aisle, past the churchgoers gawking in horrified curiosity, to the altar area.

"Please, gentlemen," Fred said as Little Bobby pursued a delighted Charlie around the altar.

"I'll take Bobby; you take Charlie," Bill said when he and Colleen reached the end of the aisle. Colleen nodded and they split up. Thanks to the presence of the reporter and cameraman, what followed next would go down in Corolla history.

Crazy Charlie, Little Bobby, and Pastor Fred chased one another in a circle at the front of the church, hopping first up then down the steps of the pulpit in cartoonlike fashion. In front was Charlie, laughing maniacally and screaming with glee every time he jumped off the platform. Hot on his heels was Bobby, slipping and sliding in his new boots and tight leather chaps. A short distance behind them came Fred, panting and snatching altar pieces before they tumbled to the ground.

Colleen positioned herself on the left side of the altar, Bill on the right. "You ready?" Bill asked her as the threesome made another loop.

Colleen gave a thumbs-up and braced herself. Charlie rounded the corner near Bill. Bill let him jump from the steps and pass by, waiting instead to grab Bobby. Colleen readied herself as Charlie made his way toward her. As he leapt up the steps, she grasped him in a hug from behind and tugged with all her might. Charlie stumbled back, peeked over his shoulder, saw Colleen, and giggled. Uh-oh, Colleen thought. The next thing she knew, her feet were off the ground and she was bouncing on Charlie's back.

"Charlie, let me down," she said with as much authority as she could muster while bobbing around.

"Giddyup, horsy! Giddyup!" he said with delight.

Colleen stole a look at Bill to see if he was making out any better. Bill was struggling to get a red-faced Bobby down on the ground in a tight hold.

"Burn burn burn! Giddyup!" Charlie yelled and galloped.

"Get out of here!" Bobby screamed and broke free of Bill.

Bobby lunged for Charlie and it struck Colleen that if she didn't think fast she'd be at the bottom of a Bobby–Charlie flesh heap. "Giddyup, horsy! Giddyup!" she shouted, slapped Charlie's backside, and held on tight.

For a second Charlie reared up and stopped. Colleen watched in dismay as Bobby reached out to attack. Just as Bobby was about to grab Charlie's shirt, Charlie let out a banshee cry and took off. Like a stallion out of the starting gate, he raced at full speed down the center aisle, Colleen holding on tight in relieved humiliation. The sunburned vacationers grinned and took pictures with cell phones; Myrtle's teaching colleagues pointed bony fingers in disapproval; and the reporter and cameraman twitched with excitement at the fact that they finally had juicy news to cover in Corolla.

As Charlie reached the back of the church, Colleen looked back in time to see, first, Bill wrestle Bobby to the ground and handcuff him, Bobby's new jeans splitting in the process; and second, Fred, arms overflowing with altar pieces, fall and rip Myrtle's portrait. There was an audible gasp from the audience, and then Colleen was carried from the building into the bright July sun.

"Okay now, Charlie, you can put me down," Colleen said as Charlie lurched around the parking lot, not knowing where "horsy" should go next.

Charlie stumbled to a halt, panting, and carefully lowered Colleen to the ground. She tugged at her uniform in an attempt to straighten her appearance and salvage any dignity she had left. Charlie, coming down from the high he had gotten from his exertions in the church, half skipped, half walked around the lot. She took a deep breath, approached Charlie, and grasped his arm to stop him.

"That wasn't very nice what you did in there," she said, gently guiding him to a bench in the shade at the side of the church.

"Little Bobby isn't nice," Charlie said.

"Bobby Crepe lost his mother. How do you think that makes him feel?"

"Happy."

"No, it doesn't. It makes him sad, Charlie, very sad," Colleen said, firmly.

"He's not sad. If he was sad, he'd cry. Little Bobby wasn't crying."

"Not everyone cries when they're sad."

"Don't you?"

"We're not talking about me."

"I ask a question so you give an answer. That's the way it works, Chief Colleen."

Colleen knew from past experience that if she didn't answer Charlie's question he'd fixate on it for the next week. "Yes, I cry when I'm sad," she said.

"Little Bobby isn't crying so he's not sad. I know he's not but you won't believe me," Charlie said in a huff and folded his arms over his broad chest.

Colleen resisted the urge to scream. What was going on to-day? She scanned the parking lot trying to figure out what to do with Charlie. Sunlight bounced off a vehicle and into her eyes. She squinted and saw the source of the reflection—Little Bobby's shiny new Harley. She stared at the Harley for a long hard moment. What if Charlie was right? What if Bobby Crepe wasn't sad about his mother's death? A new motorcycle was a strange way of showing grief. Hadn't she thought the same thing Charlie was saying though not quite in the same words?

"Tell me something," she said, trying to be patient. "Why don't you think Bobby is sad, other than because he's not crying?"

Charlie glanced at Colleen. "You believe me?"

"That depends on what you tell me. Do you know something about Little Bobby?"

Charlie nodded his head slowly up and down.

"Does it have something to do with what happened to Mrs. Crepe?"

Charlie picked at a thread on the bottom of his shirt.

"If you know something, you have to share," she said.

"Promise you won't tell?"

"You know I can't promise that if it will help Sheriff Dorman."

"Then I won't tell," he said and stuck out his lower lip in a pout.

Colleen sighed. Crazy Charlie was crazy all right . . . like a fox. He didn't leave her much choice. She'd apologize for breaking her promise to Charlie after she solved the case. "Okay," she said, wanting to cross her fingers behind her back to negate her lie.

"Say 'I promise I won't tell.'"

"I promise I won't tell. Okay?" she said.

Charlie swung his legs and kicked at the grass. After what seemed like an eternity to Colleen, Charlie muttered into his chest and was quiet again.

"What? I didn't hear you. You need to speak up."

Charlie shook his head left to right in refusal.

"Come on. I know you can say it louder than that. Don't forget, I heard you in the chapel," Colleen said and playfully poked him in the arm.

Charlie smiled and giggled. "I was loud, wasn't I?"

"Very. So why don't you tell me what happened to Mrs. Crepe . . . in your loud voice."

Colleen held her breath. She couldn't believe that Crazy Charlie might hold the key to the murder. Come on, Charlie, she thought, come on.

Charlie's grin faded. He met Colleen's eyes and simply said, "Burn burn burn."

"Burn burn burn?" she asked to make sure she had heard him correctly.

Charlie nodded.

"I don't understand. What does that mean?"

"What does what mean?" came a voice from the corner.

The reporter and his cameraman rounded the building. Great. The news media was the last thing she needed right now. The newsmen approached, the cameraman's HD camcorder tethered to the reporter's microphone. They walked in perfect synch, the cord between them maintaining the same slack.

Colleen stood to intercept them. She didn't want them anywhere near Charlie. "What can I do for you?" she asked, adopting her official fire chief persona.

"I'm Rob Anderson from WSKY Channel 4 News. I was wondering if you'd like to comment on what occurred at the memorial service or about the status of the arson investigation," the young man said. His cameraman hit the camcorder's RECORD button.

"I'm not at liberty to discuss what happened at the Crepe home. As you know, it's an ongoing investigation. As for what happened at the service, I believe you already recorded that."

"Yes, we did," the reporter said with glee. "But perhaps you could shed some light on what motivated the gentleman behind you to interrupt the service the way he did." The reporter leaned past Colleen and extended his microphone. "Sir," he said to Charlie, "why did you interrupt the service?"

Charlie's eyes darted back and forth between the reporter and Colleen like a panicked child caught dumping his meat loaf dinner in the garbage when he thought his mother wasn't watching. Colleen slowly moved her index finger over her lips to signal him to be quiet. Charlie imitated her gesture, winked, and then ran away behind the church. Yeah, Colleen thought, crazy like a fox.

"I think that means 'no comment,'" she said to the reporter and suppressed a grin.

"What about you, Chief?"

She looked straight into the camera. "I'd like to invite everyone out to the firehouse this Saturday from eight to twelve for our pancake breakfast to raise money for the junior lifeguard program. The crew will be flipping up the best pancakes on the island and giving tours of the station. And, as always, we've got Bingo Night tonight starting at eight. Thank you, Mr. Anderson, for this opportunity to speak with everyone. Now, if you'll excuse me," she said, breezed past the reporter and his cameraman, and strode toward her vehicle.

"Chief McCabe, I've got a few more questions," the reporter said as he tried to keep up, his cameraman in tow.

She picked up her pace. As she reached the middle of the lot, the doors to the chapel swung open and the bell began to toll. Colleen grinned. As she had hoped, the reporter quickly forgot about her and was now preoccupied with getting statements from mourners emerging from the church.

Bill exited and headed toward the road to direct traffic. He stopped when he reached Colleen. Would he resume their earlier conversation? "Where's Charlie?" he asked, scanning the lot.

"Charlie?" she said, temporarily thrown and a little disappointed. "Oh, he took off when the reporter started asking questions."

"I've got a few of my own to ask him," Bill said. "You okay?"

"Yeah. Why wouldn't I be?"

"You had a rough . . . ride out of the church." Bill's lip quivered and then he burst out laughing. "Giddyup, horsy," he said between chuckles.

"Stop it," Colleen said, trying to be stern but unable to contain a giggle of her own.

It felt good to laugh with Bill again. She had missed that. As it subsided, however, the awkward tension that had been between them all week returned. Bill spotted mourners getting into their vehicles and put his sunglasses on.

"Well, I'd better direct traffic."

"Right," Colleen said and forced a smile.

Bill strolled toward the road. Colleen sighed, then donned her sunglasses and strode to her SUV. She hopped in, started the engine, and pulled out before the rest of the mourners. As she approached the parking lot exit, Bill waved her out onto Corolla Village Road. She watched Bill's image diminish in her rearview mirror. She hoped at some point she could repair her relationship with him and that the rest of the day proved less eventful than the morning.

Chapter 7

"*All the 4's,* Droopy Drawers, 44!" Colleen heard Kenny Ward, one of her firefighters, cry from inside the station as she slammed her driver's-side door closed. "3-0, Dirty Gertie, blind 30! . . . All the 5's, Snakes Alive, 55!" came a second and third call as she crossed the parking lot. Colleen smiled. Kenny Ward was busy practicing his calls for their weekly Bingo Night. All had returned to normal.

Colleen avoided Kenny and instead found Jimmy working on one of the tankers around the side of the building. "Hey, Jimmy," she said, not wanting to startle him.

"Hey, Chief," he said, putting down his tools. "How was the service?"

Colleen told Jimmy about Myrtle's memorial service and her bumpy ride from the chapel, warned him that the scene would likely make the news, and told him that they should expect the press. It took Jimmy several minutes to stop laughing. She tried to appear irritated but couldn't. Jimmy's reaction was to be expected. If she hadn't been the one bouncing around on Charlie's back she'd think it was funny, too. She knew already she'd be teased by her men. There was nothing they liked better than a good ribbing.

After speaking with Jimmy, Colleen called Sparky and they quickly headed down Dolphin Street to the beach. She didn't want to be around as the story of her ride on Charlie's back spread through the station. The salt air would help her think and right now she needed to figure out how to tell Myrtle about being upstaged at her own memorial service. Besides, Sparky was happiest when he had a job to do and chasing the sandpipers would fit the bill. Sparky found the boardwalk between two beach houses and disappeared over the dunes. Colleen followed and made her way across the sand. She waved hello to one of the lifeguards and continued up the beach. Sparky galloped in front of her, his tail swinging happily in circles as he splashed after the birds.

As she passed vacationers boogie boarding in the surf, Colleen wondered what she was going to tell Myrtle about the memorial service fiasco. Normally, she'd carefully edit out the details that might cause someone pain or alarm, but she was fairly certain the entire incident had been caught on video and was currently being edited for broadcast on tonight's local news. She could naïvely hope that Myrtle wouldn't see the story, but after being cooped up at Colleen's house for a week Myrtle had become addicted to television and adept at programming the digital video recorder. Myrtle would have undoubtedly recorded any coverage her memorial service received.

Colleen had discovered Myrtle's TV addiction a few nights ago when she saw the red light on her DVR come on to signal a recording was in progress and realized Myrtle had set the machine to record a celebrity drug rehab show in place of Colleen's favorite crime drama. Myrtle had also become an expert on celebrity gossip and regaled Colleen with the details each night at dinner. If she didn't figure out soon who had tried to kill Myrtle—and succeeded in killing someone else—Colleen worried that next week Myrtle would be on her computer blogging about the trials and tribulations of being held captive by a former third-grade student nicknamed Leenie Beanie. She needed Myrtle out of her house and she needed her out pronto.

Sparky barked. Colleen squinted up the beach. The dog gingerly approached the overturned shell of a dead horseshoe crab. Sparky's head was down and cocked and his back haunches raised in true Border collie fashion. The canine inched toward the shell and pushed at it with his nose as if herding the ancient sea creature.

"Sparky, heel," she said, trying to get him away from the corpse.

Sparky responded by rolling on his back, his legs flailing happily as sand sprayed around him. Despite his disobedience, she couldn't help but smile. At least one of them was having a good time.

Colleen reached Sparky frolicking in the sand. She allowed him a few more minutes to enjoy himself, then snapped her fingers to signal it was time to return to the station. Sparky popped up and shook himself, sending sand flying everywhere. The dog was going to need a serious bath. "Sparky, station, now," she said and he took off back to the firehouse.

By the time Colleen made it to the station, she had decided that when she got home after Bingo Night she would tell Myrtle the whole bizarre story about her memorial service without any omissions. There was just no getting around the truth.

Colleen welcomed the cool air of the station and quickly bounded up the stairs to her office before any of her men saw her. She had a lot of paperwork to catch up on and e-mails and phone calls to return. She plopped into her desk chair, turned on her computer, grabbed the mound of paperwork and messages on her desk, opened a file, and began making her way through the stack.

Colleen heard the click of nails on the stairs and the panting of a hot and hungry dog. Sparky made his way to her desk and put his head in her lap. Was it time for dinner already? She glanced at the clock on her computer and was surprised to discover that several hours had passed. Bingo players would be arriving soon. She closed the folder she was working on, stretched back in her chair, and rubbed Sparky behind the ears.

"How about you and I get something to eat?" Sparky wagged his tail and trotted toward the stairs. "I'll take that as a yes," she said, stood, and followed him.

"Giddyup, Charlie!" "Yeehaw!" "When's your next rodeo, Chief?!" came the whooping calls from the firefighters as Colleen reached the first floor where the bingo tables were set up. The men laughed and hollered. Colleen felt her face grow warm and searched the room for Jimmy.

"Sorry, Chief," Jimmy said with a shrug and a smile.

"No, you're not," she said, grinning and swatting at his arm. The men were loving her humiliation and there was nothing she could do about it. It was going to be a lively Bingo Night.

She was thankful to see the first bingo players arrive. The game would take the focus off her and the chapel incident. The room soon filled up, mostly with regulars and a dozen or so vacationers. Colleen worked the crowd, greeting locals and visitors with equal regard. Bingo Night was always good for public relations.

Colleen watched Nellie enter and pause before taking a seat at the end of the table where she and Myrtle usually played together. As Colleen made her way across the room to say hello to Nellie, Bill entered. He surveyed the room and spotted Colleen. She forced a smile and a wave. He gave a slight nod before his attention was diverted by an elderly woman requesting help finding a seat.

"Are we ready for bingo?!" came Kenny's loud and enthusiastic cry. The crowd erupted in spirited cheers and a few playful jeers. Colleen grinned. No wonder Kenny lived for Bingo Night. The players loved him.

As Kenny began calling the first numbers, the players' eyes focused intently on the cards in front of them. Now would be a good time to feed Sparky and give him a bath. Colleen searched the room. No Sparky. She knelt and scanned the sea of legs under the tables.

"Looking for something?" Bill asked.

Colleen straightened. "Sparky. He's in desperate need of a bath. Have you seen him?"

Bill inspected the room. Just then a visitor entered with Sparky at his side. "I believe he's just arrived," Bill said. "And he's brought a friend."

Colleen blinked in surprise. Sparky was not prone to befriending strangers. In fact, he was typically shy with people he didn't know. The man rubbed Sparky's ear. Sparky wagged his tail with pleasure. Colleen's eyebrows raised in amazement at seeing her dog lean affectionately into the stranger's thigh.

Colleen studied the man as she crossed the room to retrieve her dog. He was rather stocky, perhaps even a little doughy around the middle. He sported a short haircut and a peculiar, wispy black mustache that didn't quite match the color or texture of his graying hair. And there was something oddly familiar about him. What was it? The hair? The posture? The clothes? Colleen took a few more steps, then stopped in her tracks. The clothes. Where had she seen that Hawaiian-print shirt and straw fedora before? It took her a second and then her mouth opened in shock. That was her father's shirt and hat from her guest room closet! The man standing in the entrance with her dog was no man at all. It was Myrtle in disguise!

Colleen stared at the disguised Myrtle in dumbfounded astonishment. The sounds of the bingo game turned to white noise. She locked eyes with Myrtle.

"Is something wrong?" Bill asked.

"What? Oh, no, I, uh . . ." Colleen said, dazed.

"You want me to take care of this?" Bill asked, his hand reflexively reaching for his gun.

"No! I mean, he's, um . . ." she stammered as, much to her horror, Myrtle approached.

"I'm her uncle," Myrtle said and thrust her hand toward Bill. "Mitch Connelly. You must be Sheriff Dorman."

"Yes," Bill said and took Myrtle's hand.

Colleen fidgeted as Myrtle vigorously shook Bill's hand. Bill smiled at Colleen, amused at the hearty handshake. She forced a weak smile in return.

"You didn't tell me you had family in town," he said.

"Yes, well, my Uncle Mitch has been staying with me. His visit was . . . unexpected."

There was an awkward moment of silence and then Bill burst out laughing. Colleen's heart sank. The jig was up. He knew it was Myrtle.

"What's so funny?" she asked, afraid to hear the answer.

"The other night . . . when I came over . . . after the fire . . ." Bill said, tears of laughter streaming down his face.

Colleen raised a quizzical brow at Myrtle. Myrtle shrugged. What was Bill finding so amusing? Then she got it. Bill was laughing because he thought the man he had heard the other night at her house was her uncle, not a romantic interest. She smiled with relief. Myrtle forced a hearty chuckle. When Myrtle's laugh got to be too much Colleen's smile disappeared, certain Bill would see through the disguise.

"I owe you an apology," Bill said. "I thought your uncle was . . . well, I thought he was a—"

"Boyfriend?" Myrtle asked. "Come on, Sheriff. You know my little Colleen hasn't caught herself a buck yet," she added, pouring on the machismo.

Colleen's eyes narrowed to slits. "Would you excuse us? I'd like a word with my *uncle*," she said through gritted teeth.

"Not at all," Bill said, grinning like the Cheshire cat. "Nice to meet you, Mitch."

"Nice to meet you," Myrtle said before Colleen dragged her outside and away from the bingo game and Bill's watchful eyes.

"Are you insane?!" Colleen asked once they were out of earshot.

"What?" Myrtle said, feigning innocence.

"What do you think you're doing? And what gave you the crazy idea to dress up in this ridiculous costume?"

"For your information, I was president of the thespian society in college. I played all the male roles. And in case you didn't notice, this ridiculous costume fooled Sheriff Dorman," Myrtle said, her fake mustache flapping with each breath.

"It didn't fool me . . . or Sparky."

"I'm tired of being locked away. There's only so much television one person can watch. When I saw the news broadcast of my service—"

"About your service—" Colleen interrupted, ready to apologize.

"What a hoot! I almost peed my pants. Can't stand those stuffy, weepy funerals. It even made the news. Wait till you see yourself bouncing around on Crazy Charlie."

"I know!" Colleen said louder than she had intended and checked to be sure nobody had heard her.

"I didn't want to miss out on any more fun so I figured out how I wouldn't have to. Remember how Sheriff Dorman thought you had a man over the night of the explosion? Well, I thought . . . what if you did? I found these clothes in a closet, cut my hair, got double-stick tape from your desk, snipped fur from Sparky and, voila, instant mustache."

"You cut Sparky's fur?" she asked, stunned.

"My hair wasn't coarse enough for a mustache. Besides, he didn't seem to mind. If you ask me, that dog needs a haircut."

Myrtle rubbed Sparky's ear. He groaned with pleasure. Colleen gave him a disapproving look. Traitor, she thought.

"Has anyone else seen you?"

"I don't think so. I found the bike in your storage shed and pedaled right over. Haven't missed Bingo Night in fourteen years."

"You're not actually thinking of staying."

"Why not?"

"Because somebody might recognize you."

"The sheriff didn't and he's the sheriff."

"Yes, well, he has a lot on his mind right now, not the least of which is trying to solve your homicide."

"I can help him—not as Myrtle Crepe, of course, but as Mitch Connelly. Being new in town, I'm free to snoop and ask questions."

Colleen considered Myrtle's plan. What her former teacher was proposing, despite the insanity of it, might just make sense. And by letting Myrtle out of the house, Colleen wouldn't have to hear any more of the celebrity gossip Myrtle had been learning about from TV programs.

"What about your name? Connelly? How am I going to explain that?"

"Simple. I'm your uncle on your mother's side."

Colleen waved a hand in defeat.

"It's settled then," Myrtle said.

Before she had a chance to stop her, Myrtle marched straight to her usual bingo table, introduced herself to Nellie, and gave a deep bow. To Colleen's amazement, Nellie actually blushed and invited Myrtle to join her. As Nellie made room for Myrtle on the bench, Myrtle winked at Colleen.

Bill joined Colleen outside. "I see Sparky's not the only one that's taken a liking to your uncle," he said, cheerfully.

"Apparently not," Colleen muttered.

"So you want help washing the dog?"

Colleen watched with dread as Myrtle helped Nellie search for the numbers on her bingo game cards.

Bill noticed Colleen studying Myrtle. "Ah, come on. Your uncle will be fine. He's with Nellie."

"That's what I'm afraid of," she said under her breath.

Colleen knew if she continued to protest her "uncle's" presence she would only succeed in drawing more attention to Myrtle. *Please behave yourself, Myrtle,* Colleen silently prayed before disappearing with Bill to the side of the building where Sparky typically got his bath.

Bill helped her drag Sparky to the plastic tub near the outdoor faucet. Sparky was a rather unflappable dog, but there was one thing he hated above all else—bath time. "Come on, you big mutt," she said, forcing him into the tub. "You sure you're up for this?" she asked Bill. "You could end up wetter than the dog."

"I can handle it," he said, happy.

Colleen twisted the faucet. Sparky made a last-ditch effort to flee before the water hit his fur and he resigned himself to the fate of becoming a clean pooch. As she and Bill lathered the Border collie, she could hear Kenny calling the bingo game. They washed the dog in silence for a while, the water slapping at the tub's edge and Sparky periodically snorting when it got too close to his nose.

"So, how's the case going?" she asked, breaking the silence.

"Which one?"

"John Doe on the beach. Myrtle's homicide. Either."

"We've got a couple leads."

"Really?" Colleen asked, hopeful.

"No."

Bill grinned mischievously. She splashed him with water. "Hey!" he said. "I thought we were washing the dog."

"We are," she said, pointedly.

Bill feigned indignant surprise and they both chuckled. It was good to be back on speaking terms.

"Seriously. How are things?" she asked as they rinsed Sparky's back and tail.

"Not so good. We've got very little evidence to go on with Myrtle's case. Your report helped with the *what* but not with the *who* of the incident. With the medical examiner's office backed up, we're stalled."

Bill fell silent and his brows furrowed. Maybe she should tell him about Myrtle. But what exactly would she say? She didn't even know what was going on herself anymore. Still, it seemed that having the three of them work on solving this together would be better than two or one. "There's something I've got to tell you," Colleen said.

"No, let me start," Bill said, interrupting. "I meant what I said. I'm sorry I jumped to conclusions about you and what turned out to be your uncle. It's none of my business who you date. I should've trusted you. You've always told me the truth. It's one of the things I value most about our friendship."

"Apology accepted," Colleen said and concentrated on washing Sparky. How could she tell him about her and Myrtle's deception now?

Bill paused in his dog-washing duty. "So, what were you going to tell me?"

"Just that if you need any help with the case, let me know," Colleen said. "Look. Sparky's done," she said, changing the subject.

Bill gave her a curious look, then smiled at the freshly washed collie. "How long before he's dirty again?" he asked, helping Colleen rub the dog down with a towel.

"I give it fifteen minutes tops," she said and released Sparky.

The dog ran a short distance, stopped, vigorously shook himself, and then ran off toward the game tables.

"Bingo!" came a cry from within the station.

"Sounds like we've got a winner," Bill said. "Shall we see who?"

Colleen and Bill headed in to check on the game. As they rounded the corner, Collen's eyes widened. Nellie was waving her hands in the air at the front of the room as Kenny inspected her card.

"Ladies and gentlemen, we've got ourselves a winner!" Kenny announced.

Nellie waved happily to Myrtle. Myrtle waved back, for a second as she normally would, then, remembering her disguise as Mitch, with a more masculine salute.

Colleen crossed to stand next to Myrtle. "How's it going, *Uncle*?"

"Just grand. Nellie won the first game," Myrtle said with pride.

"Maybe you're her good luck charm," Bill said.

"Perhaps we should be getting home," Colleen said, taking Myrtle by the elbow.

Nellie skipped to them with her winnings. "I can't believe I won. If only Myrtle had been here." Her eyes welled with tears. The group fell silent.

Colleen's heart dropped. She hated seeing Nellie upset. She hoped she didn't have to keep this charade up for long. It was too cruel.

"There, there, Nell," Myrtle said, rubbing Nellie's back. "Maybe it was Myrtle who brought you this good luck."

"No, I don't think so," Nellie said with a sniffle.

"Why not?" Myrtle asked, miffed.

"Because . . . we never won together," Nellie said and burst out laughing despite the tears.

The group stared at Nellie a moment, surprised by the sudden change in emotion. Then Myrtle joined in Nellie's laughter. Bill scratched his head, confused but amused. Colleen tried to smile but it came off as more of a snarl. Fortunately, everyone was too happy to notice.

"Would you like to join me at Big Mama's to celebrate my winnings?" Nellie asked Myrtle.

"Why, I'd be—" Myrtle began.

"I'm afraid my uncle and I need to get back home. He's had a long day," Colleen said.

"And a longer week," Myrtle said to Colleen. "It would do me good to get out."

"I can drive Mitch home," Nellie said.

Things were going from bad to worse. Colleen had to get Myrtle out of here immediately. "That's sweet of you," she said, "but I'm sure my uncle, being the gentleman that he is, wouldn't want to impose on a lady so soon after meeting her. Isn't that right, Uncle Mitch?"

Colleen glared at Myrtle, shooting invisible laser beams with her eyes. Myrtle shot back a few of her own. "My niece has a point," Myrtle said with little conviction.

"Perhaps another time then? I'll call you at the chief's house, that is, if it's okay with you, Colleen," Nellie said.

All eyes fell on Colleen. She wanted to shout, *No, it's not okay! The person you think is my uncle is really your friend Myrtle and given two more minutes with her you'll see that!*

"That would be fine," she said. "We really must be going. It's been a long day. Good night, Nellie, Bill."

Colleen guided Myrtle away from the group.

"Nice meeting you, Mitch," Bill said with a wave.

"Thank you for bringing me luck!" Nellie called after them.

"Anytime there, Nell!" Myrtle called back as Colleen dragged her around the corner to the parking lot, Sparky eagerly following behind.

Colleen opened the doors of her SUV, helped Myrtle and Sparky in, and then jumped in herself. As she started the engine, the Channel 4 news van pulled into the parking lot. She hit the gas. As the two vehicles passed each other, Myrtle leaned out her window and hollered to the reporter. "Loved your piece on the memorial service!"

"Thanks!" the reporter shouted back.

Colleen sped from the parking lot before Myrtle got them into any more trouble.

Chapter 8

"What the hell were you doing back there?" Colleen asked Myrtle as they raced away from the firehouse down Whalehead Drive.

"Watch how you speak to your uncle," Myrtle said.

"You're not my uncle or anyone else's. You're Myrtle Crepe and you almost got us into a boatload of trouble."

"I just wanted to—"

"Enough. I don't want to hear it," Colleen said, cutting Myrtle off.

Myrtle pursed her lips and stared out the passenger window. Colleen reached the end of Whalehead Drive and turned left onto Shad Street. She swung north onto Route 12, glanced at Myrtle sulking in the passenger seat, and sighed.

"You were flirting with Nellie," Colleen said after a moment's pause.

"I was what?!" Myrtle said, incredulous.

"Flirting. I saw you."

"That's ridiculous."

"You can't do that, Myrtle. You know everything about Nellie and she knows nothing about Mitch. That gives you an unfair advantage. I don't want you manipulating her so you can get out of the house."

"You don't know what you're talking about."

"Let me remind you that the reason you're in that silly disguise is because someone tried to kill you and did a good job of it to someone else. Unless you want that person to recognize you and try again, I suggest you shape up."

Myrtle tightened her lips and shifted her position away from Colleen. Colleen knew that it infuriated Myrtle to lose this argument. Still, Myrtle knew losing the argument was better than losing her life.

Colleen's attention was drawn to a motorcycle rapidly advancing from behind. She watched the rider getting closer in the rearview mirror. "Uh-oh," she said, recognizing the rider.

"What?" Myrtle asked, concerned.

Before Colleen had time to respond, Little Bobby pulled up behind them and revved his engine. Sparky sat up in the back seat and howled.

Myrtle peeked at the rider in her side mirror. "Really, now. Who raised that hooligan?" she asked in disgust.

"Yes, who," Colleen said. Normally, she would have enjoyed Myrtle unknowingly chastising herself for her childrearing skills, but right now she was worried about Myrtle recognizing Bobby.

The traffic cleared and Little Bobby moved into the oncoming lane to pass. He approached Colleen's side, gave a short wave, and roared off down Route 12. The SUV fell silent. Colleen swallowed hard. Myrtle sat pointing out the window, her mouth open in disbelief.

"Was that my Bobby?"

Colleen hesitated, then nodded.

"How long have you known about him driving around on that deathmobile?" Myrtle asked, her cheeks flushing red.

"Just since this morning. At the memorial service," Colleen said and waited for what she was sure would be a tirade.

"He rode it to my service? How could he?"

"I was going to tell you when I got home tonight but then you showed up at the firehouse and—"

"But he doesn't have that kind of money. How could he afford such a thing?"

Colleen met Myrtle's gaze. "Well," she said, carefully choosing her words, "I imagine he's accessed some of your money."

"The bank would never let him."

"They would if you were dead."

Myrtle opened her mouth but nothing came out. She glowered out the passenger-side window.

"You okay?" Colleen asked, genuinely concerned.

Myrtle shrugged. Colleen sighed. As aggravating as Myrtle was, Colleen felt empathy for her. Things couldn't have been easy this week. And now this.

"He doesn't even care that I'm gone," Myrtle said so softly Colleen almost didn't hear her.

"That's not true. He was furious at Charlie for breaking up your service."

"After all I've done for him, all I've sacrificed. This is how I'm repaid," Myrtle said with a sniffle.

Uh-oh, Colleen thought. This was beginning to sound like a pity party. It was probably the Irish in her, but one thing Colleen couldn't stand was someone feeling sorry for herself no matter how justified. She needed to snap Myrtle out of this. "Let's suppose, for the sake of argument, that Bobby doesn't seem to be grieving the way one would expect," she said.

"He's not grieving at all!"

"Everyone mourns differently. He could be in denial. Maybe getting the motorcycle is his way of avoiding dealing with the loss or making him feel alive or—"

"Spare me the psychological analysis," Myrtle said.

"Fine. Have it your way. Let's assume Bobby really doesn't care that you're gone. What does that tell us?"

"That he's an ungrateful, spoiled, shin-warming, mooch of a child!"

Now Myrtle was angry. To Colleen that was much better than a pity party. "And I'm sure you'd like to tell him that," she said.

"And then some!"

"Then we've got to find whoever tried to kill you because until we do you can't say a thing to Bobby."

"I can as Mitch Connelly."

"Stay away from Bobby, Myrtle. You hear me?"

Myrtle didn't respond.

"Listen to me. You cannot, under any circumstances, have contact with Bobby," Colleen said.

"Maybe I can, maybe I can't," Myrtle said in an almost sing-song voice.

Myrtle wasn't getting it. As much as she hated doing it, it was time for Colleen to drop the bomb. Myrtle's life might depend on it.

"Hasn't it occurred to you that Bobby could have been the one who set the fire?"

"Please. You don't know my Little Bobby. More mouse than man," Myrtle said, rolling her eyes.

"You and I both know that the most likely suspects in a crime are those people closest to the victim, usually family members. Who's the person closest to you?"

"Little Bobby?" Myrtle asked, her demeanor changing from one of condescension to one of apprehension.

"Yes," Colleen said. "Little Bobby."

Colleen and Myrtle rode the rest of the way in silence. They were both thinking about the fact that Bobby Crepe, Myrtle's son, was now officially their first suspect. Colleen tried to read Myrtle's expression but the fake dog fur mustache made it difficult. She had to give Myrtle credit. She was taking the news of her son as a suspect fairly well. Myrtle was tough and that earned her points in Colleen's book.

Colleen was relieved to arrive home. As she cut the engine and was getting out of the car, Myrtle grasped her arm.

"We have to go back," Myrtle said with urgency.

"If this is an attempt to—"

"Your bike. We left it at the station. How am I going to get around?"

"You're not," Colleen said, tugged her arm away, and jumped from the vehicle. "Come on, Sparky."

Colleen and Sparky climbed the porch steps. Myrtle slammed her door closed and marched after them.

"But Nellie already knows I'm here. I don't have to hide anymore."

Colleen shook her head in disbelief. Myrtle was like a dog with a bone. She wasn't going to let up. She faced Myrtle on the front porch. "I've had a long day. You've had a long day. Why don't we save this discussion for the morning?"

Myrtle considered Colleen's proposition for a moment. "Okay," she said and ambled to the front door to be let in.

Colleen eyed Myrtle with suspicion. That was easy. Too easy. Still, she wasn't going to question it. Whatever Myrtle's motivation for giving in, it meant they wouldn't be up all night arguing. She unlocked the door and switched on the lights. Myrtle padded into the kitchen. Smokey appeared from her hiding place in the hall closet and stretched.

"Hey, sourpuss," she said to the cat. Smokey yawned.

"Smokey, sweetie," Myrtle said from the kitchen. "Time for dinner."

Smokey perked up and bolted into the kitchen. Sparky wagged his tail and eagerly followed the cat. Colleen leaned on the kitchen entrance doorjamb. Myrtle expertly moved about the kitchen fixing Smokey dinner and giving Sparky a treat from a secret stash she had never disclosed to Myrtle. Colleen observed the activity in amazement. In one week's time Myrtle had taken over her house and her life.

"You want to watch the news? I recorded it," Myrtle said, setting the plate of food down for Smokey.

"What do you think?" Colleen asked. The last thing she wanted to do was relive the memorial service.

"Suit yourself," Myrtle said, passing Colleen on her way into the living room.

The television clicked on. Colleen headed toward the stairs and paused at the living room entrance. "Good night, Myrtle," she said.

"Good night, Chief," Myrtle said without looking away from the TV.

A slight smile formed on Colleen's lips as she mounted the stairs. It was the first time in all the years she had known Myrtle that her former school teacher had called her "Chief."

Chapter 9

Early morning. Colleen hated it when it came, but loved it once she was out of bed. Today the early rising was necessitated by a need to pick up items at the grocery store for Myrtle and get in a jog before proceeding to the station. As Colleen tiptoed down the stairs and by the living room, she was relieved to discover Myrtle still asleep on the foldout sofa. Myrtle had changed out of her disguise and was snoring softly, her mouth hanging slightly open. Smokey was curled in the crook of Myrtle's arm, her paw resting on Myrtle's chin. Colleen shook her head in disbelief at the strange bedfellows.

She made eye contact with Sparky, who popped up from his bed in the corner of the room and joined her. She grabbed her keys, wallet, and phone; quietly unlocked the door; stepped onto the porch; and gently closed the door behind her.

"Get the rabbit," she said to Sparky.

The dog took off around the side of the house in search of the rabbit that lived under Colleen's storage shed. The rabbit was Sparky's Moby-Dick. The two had been engaged in a game of cat and mouse for more than a year but the rabbit had always managed to elude his canine nemesis. If Colleen thought Sparky would really catch the rabbit she'd never give him the job. Sparky would be happily occupied with trying, though, until she returned from the grocery store.

Colleen inhaled deeply and filled her lungs with the cool, salty air. The smell reminded her of summers as a teenager when she explored the island on her bike with her best friend, Annie Michaels. The two rode everywhere, quizzing each other on the flora they had learned about in school, singing songs from favorite musicals, and stopping at the local ice cream parlor to purchase pints of mint chocolate chip and pecan ice cream, which they promptly ate from the containers.

The ice cream parlor had been a great place to flirt and giggle with boys. All the guys had liked Annie. In the summer, her dirty blond hair brightened to platinum and she tanned a flawless bronze. It didn't hurt that Annie had also been the most well-endowed girl in their class. Colleen had watched with amusement as Annie made fun of the boys and teased them. Occasionally, a boy had actually dared to approach Colleen. She remembered one in particular, Pete Fowler, who had been half her size, though that hadn't deterred him. No matter how sassy she had been or how many times she told him to go away, Pete came back for more. Eventually, Annie told Pete to scram and, to Colleen's wonder, he did. Pete and Annie had never liked each other.

Colleen grinned at the memory of Annie and Pete as she descended the porch and got into her vehicle. Little did she know those many years ago that Annie and Pete would end up married with three beautiful children. Yes, mornings like this brought back pleasant memories of the lazy summers of her youth.

Colleen sped down Route 12 to the Monteray Plaza Food Lion. She wanted to make her trip quick so she could get back before it became too hot to jog and before Myrtle had a chance to do too much snooping. In addition to basic staples, Myrtle had requested that she pick up a six-pack of Ensure, various toiletries, and a bag of pretzel sticks. Colleen added a bottle of wine to the list. Considering how things had been going lately, she had a feeling she might need it.

She passed a series of colorfully painted wooden cut-outs of horses "grazing" along Route 12. The painted cut-outs had been done by children participating in the Lighthouse Wild Horse Preservation Society's weekly Paint-a-Mustang Day. The activity was part of the Society's mission to promote awareness of and protection for Corolla's wild horses. Myrtle and Nellie had also developed activities that allowed visitors to safely meet and ride a mustang under the vigilant eyes of a preservation officer and take guided four-wheel-drive tours inside the sanctuary. These activities had done much to garner financial support, but it was the Society's efforts that led to the H.R. 306 Corolla Wild Horses Protection Act that most impressed Colleen.

Myrtle and Nellie had convinced members of North Carolina's congressional delegation that the Corolla horses needed government protection, not only because of their status on the critical lists of the American Livestock Conservancy and the Equus Survival Trusts, but because the mustangs were part of the state's heritage. A bill was proposed that would allow a herd of between 110 to 130 horses to roam free in and around the sanctuary; provide for cost-effective management of the horses while ensuring that the natural resources within the sanctuary were not adversely affected; and allow the introduction of a small number of free-roaming horses from the Cape Lookout National Seashore herd as was necessary to maintain the genetic viability of the herd in Corolla. To Colleen's amazement, when the bill came up for vote in the United States House of Representatives in early 2012, it passed without opposition. Myrtle and Nellie had taken their fight for protection of Corolla's Spanish mustangs to Washington and won. Once approved by the Senate and president, the bill would become law. When that happens, Colleen thought, it will be a day of celebration in Corolla.

Colleen reached Monteray Plaza and maneuvered her vehicle through the crowded parking lot. Vacationers and fishermen were clearly getting an early start on the day. She found a space near the Tomato Patch Pizzeria. She remembered how she had initially hated the large restaurant sign of a mustached tomato wearing a chef's hat and holding a pepperoni pizza in a white-gloved hand. She and the other islanders had grumbled for months about how tacky it was . . . until they tried the pizza. Now she regarded the sign and restaurant as one of the gems that gave the island its charm.

She parked and rushed into Food Lion. The efficient air-conditioning of the supermarket hit her like a wall of ice. She silently scolded herself for not wearing sweatpants. By the time she made it to the checkout line she'd be a popsicle. She picked up a basket and proceeded to the pet products first. Maybe she could finish shopping before her fingers turned blue.

She made her way around the store, picking up dog food, Myrtle's requests, wine, and coffee. She always picked up the milk at the end so that it wouldn't warm in the store. Not that there was any chance of that today, she thought as she grabbed two half-gallons of two-percent milk and squeezed them into her over-flowing basket. As usual, she was accumulating more items than she had expected and could have used a cart.

"Things won't be the same without Myrtle," Colleen heard someone say as she let the door to the milk section slam closed.

Sam, a former businessman who stocked the dairy section as his retirement job, approached the refrigerated shelves with a dolly filled with a yogurt shipment.

"No, they won't," she said, not wanting to get into a long conversation. Sam could spend the better part of an hour talking with just about anyone, which wasn't a problem unless that person was in a hurry.

"Nellie said Little Bobby seems to be holding up pretty well under the circumstances. Actually, I'm more worried about Nell than Bobby," he said.

"They were close," Colleen said, trying not to be rude as she inched away from the dairy section.

"Best friends since grammar school. She and Myrtle started that wild horse society together, though to hear Nell tell it Myrtle took all the credit. Man, was she bitter about that. They even had words. If you ask me, she's still a little miffed. Well, as much as she can be now with Myrtle gone."

"I didn't realize Myrtle and Nellie ever had words. It always seemed like Nellie deferred to Myrtle," Colleen said, now interested.

"Oh yeah," Sam said and leaned closer. "It was a real doozie."

"Really?" Colleen said, resting her basket on the floor.

"It happened after Myrtle caught Edna Daisey stealing the papers they keep on the horses. I don't know all the particulars but I believe Myrtle and Nellie had a difference of opinion about where the best place was to store those files. But I guess they worked it all out—like sisters do, I suppose."

"You're probably right," she said, processing this new information.

"Sam, cleanup needed in aisle five" came a voice over the store's speakers.

"I better get that," Sam said. "Nice talking to you, Miss Colleen."

"Nice seeing you again," she said and watched Sam scurry off toward aisle five.

Colleen carried her basket to the front of the store to check out. She considered the possibility of Nellie as a suspect in Myrtle's homicide. Would Nellie really kill Myrtle over matters pertaining to the Lighthouse Wild Horse Preservation Society? It didn't seem to be in her nature. Nevertheless, otherwise sane people had been known to do insane things. But even if Nellie had a motive to blow Myrtle up, it didn't seem likely Nellie would have the means. Besides, hadn't Nellie been concerned the night of the explosion about the Society's documents? Would she really blow up the house and risk losing them forever? Then Colleen remembered how passionate Myrtle had become about the documents the night before. Did Nellie feel the same way? Would she kill for them? Colleen shook her head. If she didn't watch herself, she'd think everyone in Corolla was a potential murderer. Still, if Little Bobby was a suspect because he was Myrtle's closest relative, then she'd have to rule Nellie in by virtue of the fact that she was Myrtle's closest friend. The number of suspects had just doubled.

Colleen got in line behind two fishermen at the checkout and placed her basket on the conveyor belt. She carefully opened her fingers, now stiff claws from lugging the heavy basket.

"You hear about the guy from Pennsylvania?" the fisherman with a beard asked the other.

"What guy?" the other asked.

"Heard about it last night at Joe's. Some fella comes down every year to fish and get away from the missus."

"I hear that," said the second fisherman.

Colleen and the female cashier made eye contact. Men.

"Apparently when the wife didn't get the nightly call about his daily catch she got worried. When she couldn't get him on his cell phone, she called the Bait and Tackle and Joe's to see if anyone had seen him."

"Maybe he's cheating," the cashier said, adding her two cents.

"Who would waste a week fishing messing with a woman?" the bearded fisherman said, and the two men chuckled.

The second man turned around for the first time and noticed

Colleen. She forced a smile. If only women could overhear more conversations like this, she thought. They'd certainly get a better idea about how men prioritized their lives.

"Anyways," the bearded fisherman said to his friend while handing the cashier money for the bill, "it's been two weeks and no word. Like he vanished into thin air."

Colleen suddenly perked up. Or maybe vanished into the ocean, she thought.

"If I did that to my Diane, she'd have my hide," the second man said, and whistled low imagining his wife's punishment.

"Excuse me," she said, tapping the man closest to her as the cashier handed the fishermen their receipt and began ringing up Colleen's groceries.

The men turned.

"I couldn't help but overhear your story. The man that's missing . . . do you happen to know his name?" she asked.

"No, I don't, ma'am, but I'm sure you could ask down at Joe's."

"Thank you. I'll do that," Colleen said, and gave them a reassuring smile. "Have a safe day on the water."

"Thank you," the men said in unison and walked away.

Colleen watched the men leave the store. She saw one shrug, obviously in response to the other's question: *What was that all about?* As they crossed the parking lot, however, their demeanor quickly changed and the bounce in their step returned in anticipation of catching blue marlin, Spanish mackerel, or bluefish.

Colleen's mind was awhirl. She absently paid for her groceries and left Food Lion. She had gotten more than groceries at the store. She had gotten information. Was it possible that the body that had washed up on the beach a week ago was that of the missing fisherman? Thus far, the coroner had been unable to make an identification. If the man came down alone, it would be understandable why he didn't go missing right away. Colleen would visit Joe's and see what the guys there could tell her, then call Bill and let him know that she had a lead on the John Doe from the beach.

She switched the grocery bags to one arm and reached into her pocket for her keys. She felt the contents shift and a bag slip from her grasp. Cans of dog food rolled across the pavement. She scooped up the bag and hurried to retrieve the runaway cans.

"Need help?"

"Yes," she said, grabbing another can before turning toward the voice.

Colleen froze and her knees went a little weak. Standing before her with Sparky's dog food in his hand was the handsome young man she had seen at the fireworks and the chapel.

"I believe this belongs to you," he said, his brown eyes twinkling in amusement, and handed her the can.

"Thanks" was all she could manage.

"Looks like a nice day," he said, checking out the sky.

"Yes, it should be," she said, recovering from her initial shock. "Are you staying in Corolla?"

"Visiting," he said after a brief pause.

"Friends?"

"No, family."

A horn blared behind her. Colleen jumped and swung around. A delivery driver motioned out the window of his truck for her to move. She hadn't realized she had been standing in the middle of the street. She waved an apology, stepped aside, and spotted the handsome stranger on the other side of the street on his way into the store.

"Hey!" Colleen called out.

The man turned back briefly, waved, and entered the store. She hesitated a moment. The impulsive part of her wanted to follow the man and question him further. The restrained part knew that that would seem like stalking. Her reserved side won.

She trekked toward her SUV. Why hadn't she found out who the man was staying with, or how long he was staying, or what his name was? Some detective you are, she thought. One thing she did learn was that he was visiting family, and that meant he could be in town for a while. She might discover his identity yet. She smiled at the thought. Then came questions that wiped the smile away. *Why are you really interested in that man? Do you actually think he is involved in what is going on in Corolla? Or does it have more to do with the fact that you aren't on the best terms with Bill? Perhaps you like the young man's attention.* He was certainly easy on the eyes. And was that a slight accent she detected in his rich, deep voice? Stop, she thought, unwilling to entertain what the questions implied. She reached her SUV and shook thoughts of the man from her head.

As Colleen loaded the provisions into the passenger seat, she had the feeling she was being watched. She scanned the parking lot. People were walking in and out of the store and loading groceries into trunks. Nothing out of the ordinary. But the hair on her arms stood on end, her legs felt weak, and she had a queasy

feeling in her stomach. She had had this feeling only twice before and both times her life had been in serious danger.

The first time Colleen had felt this way was in college. She had
been out with her friends from the track team and was crossing a
street when a car came screeching straight at them down the
wrong side of the road. Instead of running, her teammates had
frozen like deer in headlights. Thankfully, at the last minute the
driver had swerved and missed them. Later, the police had told
Colleen and her teammates that it was probably good they hadn't
moved, but Colleen had hated that she'd been paralyzed by her
fear.

The second time had come years later, when Colleen was
jogging through a park in Washington, D.C., after attending a
national conference of emergency service personnel. A man,
obviously suffering from mental illness, had charged at her while
brandishing a baseball bat. That time she had been able to run
away, but when she got back to the hotel she had immediately
collapsed on a sofa in the lobby.

Oddly enough, she never had this feeling while fighting a fire.
She reacted this way only when her life was threatened by another
person. She hated how her body was feeling right now but clearly
it was indicating she was in some type of danger, and she'd be
foolish to ignore it. Colleen took another look around the lot,
hopped into her SUV, and locked the door. She didn't know the
origin of the threat but decided from here on out she would be
especially careful. After all, in the span of two weeks, two people on their island were dead. She didn't want to be next.

Colleen wound down her window and felt her muscles relax

as she headed home. By the time she pulled into her driveway, she wondered if the feeling she had had in the Food Lion lot was telling her that she needed to take a vacation day. She parked in front of her house and was surprised not to find Sparky waiting for her on the front porch. Normally by now he would have worn himself out searching for the rabbit and be ready for food and a nap.

"Sparky!" she called as she grabbed the grocery bags and shuffled up the porch steps.

A distant bark was the response. Colleen's eyebrows furrowed. She cast an eye over the brush and dune grass for any sign of movement. The grass blew gently in the breeze but there were no telltale signs of canine activity or digging. She called his name again. Again she heard his bark . . . from inside the house. How had Sparky gotten in? For a second Colleen thought that someone had broken in, then recalled that Myrtle was home and had probably heard Sparky scratching at the door. Colleen inserted her key and swung the door open. Sparky greeted her, tail wagging.

"There you are," she said as she carried the groceries in and closed the door with her foot.

As she crossed to the kitchen she glanced into the living room. The sofa bed was folded and the sheets, blankets, and pillows were carefully piled on the nearby chair. Colleen had offered Myrtle the more private guest room upstairs so Myrtle wouldn't have to sleep on the couch, but Myrtle had replied that she preferred the living room because stairs gave her knees trouble. Colleen suspected that the real reason Myrtle wanted to remain on the first floor was that she had grown attached to Smokey. The two had formed a bond in the short time Myrtle had been a guest. Since Smokey wasn't allowed in the guest room because of Colleen's parents' allergies, Myrtle chose to sleep in the living room.

"I'm back," Colleen said, moving into the kitchen.

She unpacked the groceries and threw the plastic bags into a recycling bin. Sparky trailed behind. Colleen became aware of how quiet the house was. She crossed into the foyer, checked the hall bathroom, and then the back porch. No Myrtle.

"Myrtle, you better not be e-mailing on my computer," she said, advancing up the stairs.

Sparky followed, his nails clicking on the hardwood floor. She walked to her office and opened the door expecting to find Myrtle hastily logging off the computer. But the room was empty. Her heart skipped a beat. She hurried to her bedroom, as unlikely as it seemed to find Myrtle there. Again empty. The only room left was the guest room. Colleen jogged toward the room but knew with a sinking feeling that it, too, would be empty. She stood on the landing in a panic. Her pulse raced and she felt her face flush. What if the feeling she'd had in the Food Lion parking lot had been an omen? What if Myrtle had been kidnapped or worse? How would she tell Bill that the person he thought was dead was really alive and now missing?

Colleen flew down the steps two at a time. Like it or not, she had to call Bill. Time was critical in missing persons cases. She snatched the phone from the living room and dialed his number.

"Hello?" came Bill's voice on the other end.

Colleen ran her fingers through her hair. It was only then that she saw the note taped to the front of the television.

"Hello? Colleen, is that you?"

"Hey," she said, crossing to the television and removing Myrtle's note from the screen. She skimmed the message. Despite Colleen's orders against it, Myrtle had gone out.

"Is everything okay?" Bill asked.

"Yeah, fine," she said, struggling to come up with a reason for her call.

"You sure? You sound strange."

She'd have to give Bill a good reason for her call or else he'd become suspicious. "I overheard some fellas at the Food Lion talking about a missing fisherman from Pennsylvania. He may be our John Doe from the beach," she said, figuring sooner or later she was going to inform Bill.

"Did you get a name?"

"No, but apparently his wife has been calling around. I'm surprised you haven't heard. The guys said the folks at Joe's were talking about it."

"I'll check it out. Could be the lead we've been waiting for."

Colleen unfolded Myrtle's note. "Well, I gotta go. I've got a lot to do before heading in."

"Thanks for calling," he said and hung up.

Colleen read Myrtle's note again, now without the distraction of being on the phone with Bill. The note said that Nellie had called and invited "Mitch" out for pancakes. Despite her warning, Myrtle had answered the phone, accepted the invitation, and had

Nellie pick her up. Colleen wondered how Myrtle had donned her disguise, cleaned the living room, and left the house so quickly. She hadn't been gone that long.

Of course, Myrtle had made no mention of exactly where she and Nellie had gone. She knew I'd drag her back home, Colleen thought. No. Myrtle didn't want to be found. She sat on the sofa and rested her head in her hands trying to think of all the restaurants Myrtle and Nellie might go to for pancakes. Would they eat at the usual establishments? Or would Myrtle avoid those places because they would be the first places that Colleen would look? Would Nellie want to treat Mitch to something special since he was a visitor? Sparky wandered over and put his paw on her lap.

"You've got a new job," she said, rubbing the dog's ear. "Herding Myrtle."

Sparky wagged his tail. Colleen smiled. Border collies loved to work. She stood and stretched. She needed to find Myrtle and return her safely to the house before she was due at the firehouse. Her morning jog would have to wait.

Chapter 10

Where does a sixty-five-year-old woman disguised as a man with a dog fur mustache, wearing a straw fedora and Hawaiian shirt, go to eat breakfast with her unsuspecting best friend? This was the question Colleen asked herself as she sat at the end of Lakeside Drive trying to decide where she should search for Myrtle first.

After changing into work clothes and leaving a note on the refrigerator for "Uncle Mitch," Colleen had loaded Sparky into her SUV and headed out. There were several possibilities when it came to breakfast in Corolla: Big Mama's, Lighthouse Bagels and Smoothies, and First Light Breakfast and Burgers. She decided to start with Big Mama's, a favorite with the locals, and go from there.

The smells of bacon, sausage, and freshly baked muffins filled the warm morning air as Colleen pulled off Ocean Trail and entered the lot in front of Big Mama's. Her stomach growled, reminding her that she hadn't had breakfast. If it turned out Myrtle and Nellie were inside, she'd join them and grab a quick bite to eat before taking Myrtle back home.

Colleen tied Sparky up near a water dish that the restaurant had put out for dogs and went inside. Big Mama's was no-frills, with linoleum tables, a counter with stools, and a jukebox in the corner. Colleen took comfort in the fact that while the island had changed over the years, Big Mama's hadn't. The smell of coffee made her mouth water. She surveyed the small but crowded restaurant. Myrtle and Nellie weren't there.

"Morning, Chief," Al said from behind the counter.

Al "Papa" Baker had been working at Big Mama's since it opened years ago and was as much a fixture as the vinyl stools. Based on Al's size, Colleen thought he might have eaten a few too many of the restaurant's delicious baked goods over the years. The restaurant could easily have been called Big Papa's.

"Morning," she said, approaching Al. Since she was here, she might as well get a cup of coffee. The caffeine would help her think.

"Get you some java?" Al asked, reading her mind and reaching for a mug.

"Can I get it to go?"

"Coming right up," he said. He grabbed a travel cup, filled it with steaming coffee, and placed the cup on the counter. "What brings you in? We don't usually see you this early."

"I'm looking for Nellie and my uncle Mitch. They haven't been in, have they?"

"Nope."

Colleen added cream to the coffee and secured the cup's lid. "How much do I owe you?"

"After fighting that fire at the Crepe place, it's on the house," Al said and moved away to help a customer.

She took a sip. There was nothing like the sensation of the first flood of coffee over the taste buds. It filled her with renewed energy.

She left Big Mama's and unleashed Sparky. One place down, two to go, she thought. Next stop, Lighthouse Bagels. Colleen merged onto Ocean Trail. As she traveled south, she spotted Joe's coming up on the bay side. Joe's was popular with locals and sportsmen. Colleen recalled the fishermen in the grocery store talking about the missing Pennsylvania man. She slowed the SUV. Did she have time to stop and ask questions or should she let Bill handle that and continue searching for Myrtle?

As she approached the restaurant, her question was answered for her. Sitting in front of Joe's restaurant was Nellie's baby blue Buick. Nellie and Myrtle were at Joe's! Colleen scolded herself. She had guessed wrong about the breakfast venue because she had been thinking of where Nellie and Myrtle, two women, would eat breakfast, not where Nellie and her new friend Mitch would eat. She parked and cut the engine. Now if only she could get Myrtle to leave as easily as she had found her.

Colleen tied a reluctant Sparky to a post under the awning

and entered. In contrast to Big Mama's, Joe's interior was large and the décor was dark, with wood tables and chairs and a fully stocked bar at the far end. A group of men were talking loudly and imbibing at the counter. All had clearly had more than a few drinks. *And it isn't even noon,* Colleen thought. She scanned the restaurant. Joe's clientele was predominantly male, which made finding Nellie and Myrtle a piece of cake.

She spotted the two at a table, crossed the room, and put her hand on Myrtle's shoulder as she took a seat at the table. "Good morning, Uncle," she said, giving Myrtle's arm a squeeze. "Good to see you, Nellie."

"Nice of you to join us," Nellie said, pleased to see Colleen. "Isn't it, Mitch?"

"Yeah, nice," Myrtle said, forcing a smile and tugging at the straw fedora that had now become an important part of her Uncle Mitch disguise.

A waitress approached the table. "What can I get ya?" she asked Colleen while pouring her a mug of coffee.

"Blueberry pancakes with a side of bacon."

The waitress nodded. "Your orders will be right up," she said to Nellie and Myrtle and sauntered away.

"I had a tough time finding you two. You forgot to tell me in your note where you and Nellie were going, Uncle. Isn't it lucky I spotted Nellie's car out front?"

"Yes, lucky," Myrtle said without enthusiasm.

"I was showing Mitch around the island," Nellie said. "He really knows a lot about the Outer Banks. Not that I'm surprised with him being an environmental scientist and all."

Colleen studied Nellie. Was that pride on her face? It was the happiest she had seen Nellie—ever. She observed Myrtle and Nellie interacting. Could it be? Was Nellie developing a crush on her disguised best friend? This was a complication Colleen didn't need. She had to convince Myrtle to leave before Nellie saw through the disguise and got her feelings hurt.

"Unfortunately, my uncle isn't going to be staying in town too long," Colleen said. "He has a big environmental project he's been working on. Isn't that right?"

"We finished that project," Myrtle said, not going down without a fight.

"Really? Because I got a call this morning from your office and they said they needed some follow-up data from you."

"Oh, that really would be too bad if you had to leave so soon," Nellie said.

Colleen and Myrtle squared off like gunslingers at high noon. Nellie eyed the two, sensing—if not understanding—the tension between them.

"If you two will excuse me, I'm going to go powder my nose."

Myrtle rose, pulled Nellie's chair out, and tipped her hat before Nellie walked away.

"This is too much, Myrtle," Colleen said when Nellie was gone.

"I told you I was a good actress," Myrtle said, not the least bit worried. "You're the one that's going to blow it."

The waitress arrived with their breakfast orders. Colleen had more to say to Myrtle but right now the pancakes were calling to her. Just one bite and then she'd get Myrtle to see that what she was doing was not only wrong but dangerous. Colleen took a bite of the pancakes. Hot blueberries burst in her mouth. She chewed and washed the food down with a sip of coffee.

A shaft of light filled the restaurant as the front door opened and Bill entered. "Crap," Colleen said under her breath.

"There's no need to swear at me," Myrtle said, indignant.

"Hush," she said, slouching in her chair. If Bill saw her in Joe's he'd think she had been asking questions about the missing fisherman behind his back . . . and he'd see Myrtle. Colleen didn't think Myrtle could fool Bill with her disguise a second time.

Bill crossed to the bar and took a seat at the counter. "Don't turn around," she said to Myrtle, keeping her own face down.

Of course, Myrtle did exactly that. Nellie exited the ladies' room and, to Colleen's dismay, tapped Bill on the shoulder and pointed to Colleen. Bill swiveled and locked eyes with her. Please don't get up, Colleen silently prayed. Bill got up. Please don't come over here, she prayed again. Bill headed toward her and Myrtle.

"They're coming this way," she said to Myrtle under her breath. "Let me do the talking."

Myrtle drew her hat down to hide her face. Nellie and Bill arrived at the table.

"Look who I found," Nellie said.

Colleen smiled weakly at Bill.

"Care to join us, Sheriff Dorman?" Nellie asked.

"I'm sure the sheriff has a lot to do today," Colleen said.

"Don't mind if I do," Bill said, sitting opposite Colleen.

What a nightmare, Colleen thought. She had to get Myrtle out of Joe's without simultaneously hurting Nellie's feelings and arousing Bill's suspicions. It would be tough, but she could do it—if Myrtle kept her mouth shut.

"Morning, Sheriff," Myrtle said with a grunt.

Colleen wanted to scream. Hadn't she just told Myrtle to let her do the talking?

"Good morning," he said, his eyes fixed on Colleen. "You didn't mention you were taking your uncle to breakfast at Joe's."

"Colleen didn't know we were here," Nellie said before Colleen could reply. "She happened to see my car out front. Isn't that a happy coincidence?"

"Yes, it is," Bill said, skeptical.

The waitress strutted to the table and stood close to Bill—too close, if you asked Colleen. "Can I get you the usual, Sheriff?" she asked with a purr.

"Just some coffee, Becky," he said with a smile.

"Not even a piece of pie? I can't have you getting skinny on me," Becky said and flirtatiously poked at his middle.

"Maybe next time," Bill said with a chuckle.

"You let me know if you change your mind," she said and sashayed away, hips swinging with added vigor.

Colleen stared at Bill with a raised brow. His smile disappeared and his cheeks flushed. She stabbed at her pancakes, took a bite, and chewed.

When Colleen got angry, she got hungry. The first time she had realized this was when she was thirteen. She had called a boy she had a crush on to ask him to the school's Sadie Hawkins Dance. The entire concept of the Sadie Hawkins Dance—girls asking boys—seemed backward to her but she wanted to go, so she picked up the phone and made the call. The boy's sister had answered and when Colleen had said why she was calling there was a long muffled pause. Then the sister had told Colleen that her brother wasn't home. The problem with that answer was that the sister hadn't covered the receiver enough and Colleen had heard the boy in the background telling his sister that no way, no how did he want to go to the dance with "Leenie Beanie Mc-Cabe." After she had hung up, Colleen had proceeded to eat an entire loaf of banana bread that her mother had baked that morning. Not surprisingly, the pancakes on her plate were now gone. Good thing she had a fast metabolism.

"So, Mitch, how are you enjoying Corolla?" Bill asked, breaking the tension.

"It's real nice," Myrtle said, keeping her head down.

"Mitch knows so much about the Outer Banks. It's like he grew up here," Nellie said.

"Really?" Bill said, now turning his full attention on Myrtle.

Uh-oh, Colleen thought. She knew that look. It's the one Bill turned on suspects when he was about to interrogate them. Many had withered and crumbled under his questioning.

"I was wondering, Mitch," he said, "what was Colleen like as a kid?"

"We don't need to bore everyone with stories about me," Colleen said.

"I wouldn't be bored. Would you, Nellie?"

"Not at all."

Everyone focused on Myrtle. Nellie waited with polite interest,

Bill with delighted anticipation, and Colleen with growing dread. A moment passed. Colleen silently pleaded with her eyes for Myrtle to keep quiet. Myrtle grinned and leaned toward Nellie and Bill. Colleen's heart sank. Myrtle was going to do it. She was finally going to have her revenge on Colleen and reveal every embarrassing, silly thing she had done while a student in Myrtle's third-grade class.

Colleen wondered what stories Myrtle would share. Maybe she'd tell them about the time Colleen put a rubber frog on Myrtle's seat. Well, that wouldn't be too bad. Or the time she got in trouble for laughing at a kid who made fart sounds with his underarm. Still not too bad. Or perhaps it would be the time Colleen stole the chalk so Myrtle couldn't write their math test on the board. The possibilities were endless. Whatever it was that Myrtle selected, Colleen had always known this day would come.

"You want to know what Colleen was really like as a girl?" Myrtle asked, pausing for dramatic effect.

Colleen closed her eyes. She heard her heart beat in her ears.

"She was always the bright spot of my day."

Colleen opened her eyes, stunned.

Myrtle winked. "She kept me on my toes."

"Spoken like a proud uncle," Nellie said, clutching her napkin to her heart.

Colleen didn't know whether to laugh or cry. She wanted to hug Myrtle until her silly dog fur mustache fell off. Instead, she calmly turned to a disappointed Bill and said, "See?"

"She's still keeping us on our toes," he said with a grin.

Colleen swallowed with relief. One disaster averted. She checked her watch. She was due at the station in five minutes. Now was the time to get Myrtle out of there before her luck changed. "Nellie, I hope you don't mind, but I was hoping to steal Mitch away and show him around the firehouse today. I'm due there in five minutes," she said.

Nellie's eyes showed disappointment but she put on a brave smile. "I understand. Perhaps we'll get together later, Mitch?"

Myrtle glanced at Colleen. "Perhaps," she said.

Colleen rose, removed money from her wallet, and dropped it on the table. "This one is on me, folks. Shall we, Uncle?"

Myrtle reluctantly stood, tipped her hat to Nellie, shook Bill's hand, and proceeded toward the exit. When Colleen reached the front door she stole a look at Nellie and Bill. They were watching her and Myrtle and waved. Colleen waved back, then escaped into the bright light of the parking lot.

Colleen inhaled deeply. They were safe. For now, anyway. She knew it was only a matter of time before she'd have to tell Bill about Myrtle. But she needed evidence or a lead in Myrtle's case. Without evidence, she'd have nothing to offset their deception. That meant only one thing. She'd have to go see Pinky. He was the only person who might know the identity of one of her suspects—the gunman she saw at the Lighthouse. But first she had to check in at the station.

Colleen unleashed Sparky from the post, opened the SUV doors for Myrtle and Sparky, slid into the vehicle, and started the engine. "So I was a bright spot, huh?" she asked Myrtle with a grin.

"Don't let that go to your head, Leenie Beanie," Myrtle said.

Colleen beamed and pulled onto Ocean Trail.

Chapter 11

Colleen drove to the station giddy with the knowledge that Myrtle had begrudgingly admitted to liking Colleen when she had been a student in her class. "You could have told Bill and Nellie any number of stories about me," she said with a grin.

Myrtle rolled her eyes. "I didn't tell them stories because, like it or not, we're a team. And teammates stick together. That and . . ." Myrtle's voice trailed off.

"That and what?"

"That and you're the only person I know for sure isn't a suspect in my murder."

"How do you know I'm not?" Colleen said, trying to sound menacing.

"Please. You wouldn't hurt a fly."

"What about when I hit Richie Robinson during morning recess?" she asked, recalling how much trouble she had been in with her parents after the incident. She didn't consider herself a mean person but she didn't like the idea that Myrtle thought of her as a weak, do-nothing either.

"You only did that because Richie was pummeling the Jenkins boy to get his lunch money," Myrtle said in her matter-of-fact teacher voice. "That Jenkins boy should have been sticking up for himself. Imagine letting a girl take on your battles. You were always for the underdog, even when the underdog didn't deserve it."

It was true. When Colleen was five she had stood up to a group of boys twice her age who had been picking on a stray cat. It was the first time she could remember feeling angry at seeing the helpless or disadvantaged bullied. The boys had pushed her around a bit but the cat had managed to escape. She considered it a victory and in the days that followed wore the bruises she had suffered like badges of courage.

Much to her mother's consternation, Colleen's championing of the underdog had continued into high school when she brought home a series of friends her mother had called her "stray cats" or "projects." Even when the stray cats had done things Colleen didn't think were right, she had excused them because of their misfortunes or family troubles. She could still hear her mother's warning: "No good deed goes unpunished." To Colleen's great disappointment, her mother's warning had proven true on numerous occasions. She hoped her present situation with Myrtle wasn't one of them.

She arrived at the firehouse and parked. She didn't, however, cut the engine. "We need a game plan before we go in," she said, turning to Myrtle.

"What do you have in mind?"

"You say as little as possible, for starters."

"Aren't people going to find it strange that you have a mute uncle?" Myrtle asked sarcastically.

"Given your appearance, the fact that you don't speak will be the least strange thing about you."

"I happen to think that Mitch Connelly is a rather dapper fellow," Myrtle said, insulted.

Colleen gave Myrtle the once-over. Okay. Maybe to a woman of a certain age Myrtle was dapper. At least Nellie seemed to think so. "Promise me you won't say too much."

"I don't make promises," Myrtle said.

Colleen threw her hands up in defeat and cut the engine. She didn't have time for Myrtle's games. She had to make an appearance inside or her staff would wonder what she was doing out in the parking lot. She didn't know why she had even tried. Myrtle was going to do what Myrtle wanted and there was nothing she could do about it. She opened her door.

"Wait," Myrtle said.

Colleen paused, low on patience.

"As you wish," Myrtle said and made a gesture of locking her lips and throwing away the key.

"Thank you."

Today was actually a good day for Colleen to show Myrtle around. Starting mid-June and ending mid-August, the Whalehead Ocean Rescue team ran the Safety Education and Aquatic Learning for Kids program, otherwise known as SEAL Kids. SEAL Kids was a free ocean safety mini-camp designed to teach children ages seven to fourteen about ocean conditions, how to recognize an emergency, how to summon help, and general physical fitness. She was proud of how the program had grown over the years, thanks in part to local business sponsors such as Salvatore Development Corporation, which enabled the program to remain free to anyone who signed up. It was a valuable and proactive public service and one that Colleen logically would show off to her uncle.

She checked in with Jimmy at the station, briefly introduced her uncle Mitch to the guys, and headed out to the beach where the SEAL Kids class was conducted. Since Myrtle had been a schoolteacher, Colleen thought she might enjoy seeing the kids. It would also keep Myrtle out of the station and away from the curious eyes of her staff.

Colleen, Myrtle, and Sparky strolled up the road to the wooden ramp directly across from the lifeguard station. They marched up the boardwalk and over the dunes. Down the beach, Colleen spotted two Ocean Rescue instructors with a group of kids. The instructors had set up small orange cones and had divided the kids into teams. These teams were now cheering and running in a shuttle race between the cones. Colleen smiled at their enthusiasm.

"I thought you'd like to see the kids," she said to Myrtle.

"Haven't I seen enough in my day?"

Colleen raised her brows in surprise.

Myrtle shrugged. "You try teaching grade school for thirty-five years."

Just then, three horses plodded over a dune several hundred

yards up the beach. Sparky tilted his head to the side, lifted an ear, and took off running.

"Sparky, no!" Colleen called, but it was too late.

The Border collie was doing what he was bred to do—herd. She hoped he didn't nip at the horses' back hooves too much. In the past, when he had approached the horses too closely from behind, the horses had kicked at him to drive him away. On rare occasions the horses had connected with Sparky's body, but never harshly enough that it prevented Sparky from coming back for more. One thing about Border collies, they were hardy, persistent dogs.

Sparky dipped his head and darted among the horses. The horses moved right then left. Sparky followed their movements in an intricate dance. Colleen was relieved to see that today the horses didn't seem to mind the pesky dog. Instead, they wandered to the wet sand, Sparky at their heels.

"He'll come back, won't he?" Myrtle asked.

Colleen smiled. There was genuine concern in Myrtle's voice. "Border collies stick to their territory. He'll come back when he's gone too far. Shall we see what the kids are up to?"

"If we must," Myrtle said, and followed her across the sand toward the students in the SEAL program.

"Morning, Chief," one of the instructors said as they approached. "Kids, I'd like to introduce you to Chief McCabe."

"Good morning," Colleen greeted the dozen or so children squinting up at her.

"Good morning," they said in unison.

"You're the fire chief?" a little boy with red hair and burned cheeks asked.

"That's right."

"I didn't know girls could be fire chiefs," he muttered, wrinkling his nose.

"Young man, girls can be anything they want," Myrtle said in her Mitch Connolly voice.

"Sorry, sir," the little boy said.

Some in the group, mostly the girls, giggled. Colleen suppressed a smile. Myrtle hadn't lost her touch with children.

"Okay, that's enough," one of the instructors said.

The kids obediently fell quiet. Colleen had to hand it to the Ocean Rescue instructors—they ran a tight ship.

As one of the instructors was about to begin the next part of the mini-camp, a lanky girl of about ten years of age, with frizzy hair and braces, came running at them from down the beach. "Hey!" she yelled as she ran, her arms waving wildly. All eyes watched the girl as she sprinted through the dry sand, ponytail flapping erratically up, down, and sideways. She reached the group, flushed and out of breath.

"What is it, Ashley?" an instructor asked, alarmed.

"I think I spotted an emergency," she said between gasps.

Everyone scrutinized the ocean, expecting to see a swimmer in need of help in the surf but saw a line of pelicans gliding over the breaking waves instead.

"Take a breath and tell me what you saw," the instructor said.

Ashley did as instructed, gulping in so much air Colleen thought she'd pass out. Finally, the girl pointed to the dunes up the beach. "There was a man. He was digging."

"A lot of people dig in the sand. We're at the beach," the second instructor said.

The children giggled. Colleen and Myrtle were not amused. Not too long ago a body had turned up on the beach.

Colleen knelt beside the girl. "I'm Chief McCabe with the fire department. You want to tell me what you saw?"

"Chief, that's really not necessary," one of the instructors said, obviously mortified that his boss's time would be taken up by an overzealous pupil.

"It's fine," she said.

Colleen put her arm gently on the girl's shoulder and guided her away from the group. "This is my uncle," she said as Myrtle joined them. "Why don't you show us where you saw the man digging."

The girl eyed Myrtle somewhat warily but bobbed her head and began hiking through the dry sand toward the dunes. As Colleen and Myrtle followed, the girl between them, they looked at each other with apprehension.

"He was right over here," Ashley said, making a move to climb the dune.

Colleen touched the girl's arm to stop her. She didn't know if there was anything to the girl's story but if it was linked to the body that had washed up earlier or the explosion at the Crepe house, she didn't need the child traumatized by seeing a dead body buried in the dunes.

"Tell me about the man. What did he look like?" she asked.

The girl cocked her head to the side, thinking for a second. "He had black hair and black eyes. When he saw me watching him he made a fist and shook it at me. Then the dog came and barked and he ran away."

"What did the dog look like?" she asked, scanning the beach.

"Black and white with a big fluffy tail," Ashley said, smiling.

"Sparky," Myrtle said, voicing Colleen's own thought.

"Did the dog run after the man?" she asked.

Ashley nodded. "They went over the dune."

Colleen's heart raced. It was unusual for Sparky to run after someone unless he was feeling threatened or protecting his territory. If the man was the person who had burned and dumped the body that had washed up on the beach, she had no doubt he'd harm a dog.

"Ashley, I want you to stay here with my uncle," Colleen said. "Sparky!" she called as she ascended the dune.

Colleen whistled several short blasts, which she did only in times of emergency. What if something had happened to Sparky? She fought back tears, trying not to jump to conclusions. Her breathing grew labored as she plowed her way to the top of the dune. As she reached the peak, Sparky came bounding up from the other side, his tongue out and his tail wagging.

"That's him!" the girl yelled from below.

"Sparky!" Colleen said, embracing the dog and collapsing in the sand.

The dog rolled in the sand, delighted that he had played such a good game of hide-and-seek. Colleen had been warned when Sparky was a puppy that Border collies had a mischievous side and could be intentionally defiant in an attempt to get their owners to chase them or play. This was the first time such behavior had panicked her, and she rubbed his chest with relief.

"No treats for you, mister," she said, not really meaning it. "Heel," she said, then stood and pointed to the beach below.

Instead of obeying, the dog loped to the top of the dune and disappeared from sight.

"He's a bad dog," said the girl with delight.

"No, young lady, he's a smart dog," Myrtle said.

Colleen and Myrtle locked eyes. Maybe there was a reason Sparky had followed the man. After all, this part of the beach was beyond his usual territory.

"I'm going to check it out," she said to Myrtle and slogged up the dune.

Colleen reached the top and half expected to see a dead body waiting for her on the other side. Instead, Sparky was busily digging in a section of the dunes hidden from view by a thick cluster of grass. Colleen carefully made her way down the other side of the dune, conscious of how delicate the dunes and the grass that grew on them were.

As she descended, half stepping, half sliding, the ocean breeze diminished and the temperature increased. Perspiration dotted her upper lip and forehead. She wiped both with the back of her hand as she reached Sparky. The dog was digging furiously but not making much progress. As soon as he cleared sand away, more filled the hole.

"What have you got there?" she asked, nudging him aside.

The canine watched intently as Colleen took over digging.

She had the same difficulty as Sparky with sand instantly filling in the hole where she dug. Unsure of what she would find, she gave up and pushed her hand deep into the dune. She stretched and wiggled her fingers, feeling for something, anything. She stopped when she felt smooth plastic around what felt like a brick.

Colleen extracted the item and sat back. The object was a tightly wrapped parcel with a dark brown substance inside. The outer plastic had been stamped with the product logo HOT SAUCE. Colleen instantly used the bottom of her shirt to hold the package. If she was right about the contents, the police would want to dust the casing for fingerprints. The less she contaminated the object with hers the better.

Sparky reclined in the sand, sphinxlike, and grinned at her. Colleen rubbed his ear. He had done well. She reached into her pocket and removed her cell phone. She couldn't keep Bill in the dark any longer. The stakes were too high.

Bill answered on the second ring. "Hey," he said, knowing it was her from his caller ID.

"Can you meet me on the beach near Shad and Lighthouse?" Colleen asked, not wanting to get into too much detail until she saw him in person.

"What's up?" he asked. "Things are a little busy here."

"It's not a body, but a girl and Sparky found something in the dunes."

"I'll be right there," he said.

"And Bill?"

"Yeah?"

"You'll want to bring your people."

Colleen hung up. She hoped the bundle was enough evidence to keep Bill from hauling her and Myrtle into the police station for obstructing the investigation of Myrtle's death.

She rose and brushed herself off. She'd better tell Myrtle that Bill was on his way. She ordered Sparky to stay where he had been digging. He gladly obliged. She reached the dune's crest and waved to Myrtle and the girl.

"Is everything okay?" Myrtle asked, uneasy.

"We're gonna have company," Colleen said.

Chapter 12

"Have you lost your mind?" Bill asked, trying unsuccessfully to keep his voice down.

Bill's deputies and the Drug Enforcement Administration agents working in the cordoned-off area of the dune eyed Bill and Colleen, who were standing several yards away on the beach below. Colleen squinted up at them. Bill forced a smile and waved. The agents resumed their excavation and crime scene investigation. Thus far, they had uncovered twenty bricks of heroin in addition to the one Colleen had unearthed.

"If Myrtle is alive, where is she?" Bill asked in a lower voice.

"Follow me."

"No games, Colleen," he said, holding his ground. "Where is Myrtle Crepe?"

She checked to be certain they weren't being observed and

leaned closer lest the ocean wind carry her voice over the dunes to the ears of the crime scene investigation team.

"She's up the beach with Sparky and the girl," she said. "The girl said she won't talk to anyone but me and the only reason she's doing that is because she likes Sparky. Please, you can yell at me later, but right now I need you to come with me."

Colleen waited. Later, she'd take whatever consequences her friendship would suffer from having concealed Myrtle's status as a living being, but right now the most important thing was protecting the girl and Myrtle. That meant Bill needed to accompany her away from the alert eyes of investigators and curious vacationers.

Bill was furious. But she could see from the way his eyebrows came together in a furrow above his nose that behind his anger was concern. She proceeded up the beach, hoping he would follow. A moment later, he was at her side.

They walked in silence. Colleen understood she'd have to answer a million questions. She dreaded Bill's interrogation but on some level thought she deserved it. They arrived at the dune behind which Myrtle and the girl were hidden with Sparky. Colleen glimpsed down the beach to be certain they couldn't be seen. Due to a bend in the beach, she and Bill were well out of sight of the investigators.

"This way," she said.

She led the way into the dunes, tracking the footprints she, Myrtle, the girl, and Sparky had made earlier when they found the hiding place. They tramped through beach grass, onto a lot where a house was partially under construction, and into a deserted construction area.

"So where is she?" Bill asked.

Colleen gave a short whistle. Sparky ran from behind what would eventually be the ground-floor storage area of the house. The girl peeked around the corner.

"It's okay, Ashley," Colleen said in a soothing voice. "See? Sparky likes Sheriff Dorman."

Bill played along and rubbed Sparky's ear. Sparky wagged his tail, fell to the ground, and rolled onto his back. Ashley smiled, joined them, and dropped to her knees to rub Sparky's belly.

"Where's my uncle?" Colleen asked the girl.

Ashley pointed behind her while stroking the dog. Colleen met Bill's eyes and gave a quick nod toward the house.

"What about the girl?" he asked in a whisper.

"She's with Sparky. She'll be fine," Colleen said and continued toward the partially constructed residence.

A completed first floor and the skeleton of a second floor sat on pylons. It was obvious from the number of support posts and the size of the concrete slab that the completed house would be one of the many mansions that were becoming increasingly popular oceanfront property.

"Looks like a Pinky Salvatore special," Bill said with disapproval.

The house groaned in the wind as if responding to what Bill had said. Colleen held her tongue. It was better not to say anything right now. Bill was angry enough. She crossed the lot until they were under the first floor.

"Myrtle?" she said.

They walked around a corner and toward what would be the front portion of the house. Myrtle stepped from behind a pillar. Bill stopped in his tracks. She joined Myrtle. It was better for them to take the heat together.

Bill studied Myrtle a long while. "How could I not have seen it," he said.

"Myrtle *was* president of the thespian society in college," Colleen offered, sensing his mortification.

"What? She throws on a hat and mustache and suddenly she's a different person?"

"In all fairness," Myrtle said with unusual gentleness, "you weren't looking for it."

"What kind of cop misses this?" Bill asked, gesturing at Myrtle. "It's like not recognizing Clark Kent is Superman."

Bill spun away and put his hands on his hips. Colleen and Myrtle looked at each other with worry. Bill felt duped and the deception had wounded his law enforcement ego. Colleen could handle him being angry at her, but the thought that he doubted his professional skills was unbearable. He was the most astute police officer she knew, because he kept his eyes and ears open.

Colleen understood Bill well enough to know that his slouched shoulders meant he was chastising himself for allowing his personal feelings and relationship with her to interfere with the investigation. He had trusted her and she had betrayed that trust. It was quite possible that after this stunt she might never get it back again.

"I'm sorry," she said. "I wanted to tell you."

Bill straightened his back. "I need to talk to the girl."

"Of course," she said but her heart sank. Bill had let their relationship cloud his judgment. He wasn't going to let that happen again. From here on out he'd be all business. Myrtle and I are slugs, Colleen thought before summoning the girl.

"Ashley," she said, peeping around the side of the house. "Would you mind joining Sheriff Dorman and me?"

Ashley rubbed Sparky's belly.

"You can bring Sparky."

Ashley patted Sparky's head. "Come on, doggie."

The girl and dog united with the rest of the group. Having Sparky with them was a godsend. He's going to get as many treats tonight as he likes, Colleen thought as they assembled under the house.

Colleen knelt next to the girl. "Tell Sheriff Dorman what you told us about the man on the dune."

Ashley glanced up at Bill, then down at Sparky. Bill stooped so as not to tower over the child and Myrtle backed away to give them more space. The ocean breeze blew through the skeletal wood structure, causing floorboards not fully secured to squeak and groan.

"It's okay," Bill said. "You're not in trouble. Just tell me what you told Chief McCabe and her"—he paused before finishing—"uncle."

Colleen and Bill waited. The girl massaged Sparky's ears.

"I saw a man digging," Ashley said.

"Can you tell me what he looked like?" Bill asked.

"Scary."

"Scary how?"

The girl shrugged. "Just scary."

"If we went to the station do you think you could describe the man so we could get someone to draw a picture of him?"

The girl stopped stroking the dog. The house creaked above them. Colleen shifted her attention to the ceiling. The wind died down and all went silent. She refocused on the girl.

"Ashley?" Colleen said. "Do you understand what the sheriff is asking?"

"Uh-huh."

"Do you think you could do that for us?"

"I don't want to go to the station."

"We'll call your parents and they can meet us there. How about it?" Bill asked.

Ashley shook her head. Colleen could see the frustration on Bill's face. He was having a hard time with the opposite sex, old and young.

"The only way we can keep the man from scaring anyone else is if you help us figure out what he looks like," Colleen said. "The sheriff has an artist who can draw the man's face."

"Miss Kennedy can draw," the girl said, brightening.

"Who's Miss Kennedy?" Colleen asked.

Ashley beamed. "Miss Kennedy is my art teacher at school. She's really nice."

Colleen glanced at Myrtle for verification. Myrtle nodded confirmation.

"Miss Kennedy says she likes how I use color on my art projects," the girl said with pride.

Bill exhaled. Colleen knew he hated involving the art teacher but it seemed like it was the only way they were going to get a sketch of the suspect.

"So if Miss Kennedy agrees, you'll help her draw a picture of the man?" Bill asked.

Ashley nodded. Like it or not, Bill had to involve the teacher in the case.

"I'll get my vehicle," he said, the reluctance heavy in his voice.

Bill strode toward the beach. He reached the edge of the cement pad. "Everyone stay put," he said, then made his way back over the dunes.

It didn't take Bill long to return with his SUV. He surveyed the street before signaling Colleen to bring Myrtle, the girl, and Sparky out from hiding. They squeezed into the vehicle, Colleen riding up front with Bill and the other three riding in the back.

As he steered the car south, Colleen absently noted a charcoal-colored sedan parked on the shoulder in the sand thirty feet away. Corolla had public beach parking but still some visitors insisted on leaving their vehicles on private property and dunes. *They want the private beach experience without paying the private beach rental,* she thought. As they rounded the bend in the road, her attention shifted back to the present situation.

"I called Miss Kennedy," Bill said, stealing a peek at the girl in the rearview mirror. "We're going to her house. Your parents are meeting us there."

"I've never been to a teacher's house," Ashley said in awe.

Colleen and Myrtle grinned.

The group rode the rest of the way in silence, traveling south on Route 12 into Duck. Each was preoccupied with his or her own thoughts. Colleen's mind turned to the firehouse. Her employees would worry if she didn't check in soon. Once they reached their destination and the girl began working with her teacher on the sketch, Colleen would call the station to give Jimmy an update. She stared out the passenger-side window and attempted to formulate a duty list for Jimmy, but her mind kept drifting back to her concern for Ashley and Myrtle. Even though Bill was angry with her, Colleen was relieved that he knew Myrtle was alive and that she no longer had to carry the burden alone.

Chapter 13

Colleen sighed with relief as Bill entered Miss Kennedy's Currituck Sound neighborhood. It had been an uncomfortable, quiet ride and she was eager to see it come to an end. As they approached, all eyes widened at the sight of the art teacher's house. Several dozen bicycles painted entirely white substituted for a picket fence around the pale yellow rambler. Blue glass bottles dangled from tree limbs. Bed frames overflowing with black-eyed Susans and cosmos served as flower beds.

"Wow," Ashley said as Bill cut the engine.

"Artists," Myrtle said with a *tsk*.

Colleen frowned at Myrtle as she and Bill exited the front of the vehicle and helped the others from the back.

"Can the dog come?" Ashley asked.

"How about if Sparky stays on the porch while you and Miss Kennedy work," Colleen said.

The girl nodded once, as if that made perfect sense, and bounded toward the house. The front door flew open and Ashley's parents rushed out. "You okay, Ash?" the father asked, inspecting his daughter.

"Yeah," Ashley said, annoyed by his examination.

The girl's parents each took one of Ashley's hands. "How long is this going to take, Sheriff?" the father asked.

"Just until we get a sketch. Then you're free to take her home."

"Ash, why don't you go inside with Mommy while I talk with the sheriff? I think Miss Kennedy has some lemonade for you."

"Mind if I join you?" Myrtle asked.

"Not at all," the girl's mother said and the three disappeared inside.

Colleen settled Sparky on the porch near an old tuba with morning glories climbing from its bell.

"Is my girl in some type of danger?" the father asked Bill when his wife and daughter were out of earshot.

"I'll post a man at your house. It's probably best if she doesn't go out by herself," Bill said.

"What exactly did Ashley see?"

"As far as we know, just a man digging," Colleen said, descending the porch steps to join them.

"What's the big deal about a man digging at the beach?"

"It's what he was digging for that's the big deal," Bill said. "I'm afraid I can't disclose anything further and I'd prefer if you didn't try to question Ashley too much. She'll probably get a lot of that from investigators. The best thing you can do is continue as you would in your daily routine."

The father rubbed his chin. Colleen wished they could tell the man more, but Bill was right. It was safer for the girl and her family if they didn't know about the heroin until the federal agents felt the family was safe from whatever criminal organization was responsible for importing the Schedule 1 substance. Based on the product logo on the package, Colleen suspected the heroin had come from Mexico or Colombia.

Despite the likely South American source of the illegal drugs, Colleen couldn't help but wonder if Pinky was somehow involved. Myrtle had suspected Pinky of being part of the Mafia; and the Mafia had a history of heroin trafficking in the United States that dated back to the late 1940s. But even if Pinky was involved, why bury the heroin in the dunes? It hardly seemed like a safe place for such a valuable, albeit illegal, commodity. The only thing Colleen could think of was that it had been a temporary drop location or that a transaction had somehow been interrupted and the dune was a quick place to dump the drugs.

"Let's go inside," Bill said.

Colleen, Bill, and Ashley's father moved toward the house. Sparky woofed once, wanting to follow. "Hush," Colleen said and pointed to the ground for him to lie down.

The dog reluctantly obeyed as Bill and the father disappeared inside the house. Sparky laid his head down, then picked it up again as a charcoal-colored sedan slowed in front of the house. Colleen searched for what had attracted his attention and saw the sedan disappear down the street.

"Colleen?" Bill asked from the doorway.

"I'm coming," she said and entered the house.

Colleen and Bill joined the others in the kitchen. Ashley's mood had picked up considerably. She had an empty glass on the table in front of her and her teacher next to her. Miss Kennedy was everything Colleen expected, with frizzy red hair streaked with strands of gray and pinned up in a loose bun by two purple pencils. She wore a multicolored caftan over a long, flowing cotton sundress, practical brown sandals, a crystal around her neck, and several rings on each hand.

"I was looking for shells to draw, like you told me in class, when I saw the man, Miss Kennedy."

Miss Kennedy smiled warmly. "More lemonade?"

"Yes, please," Ashley said and pushed her glass toward her teacher.

"Can I get anything for anyone else?" the teacher asked as she poured Ashley another glass. The group declined. "Very well. Shall we get started then?" she asked Bill.

"Ready when you are."

"So," the teacher said to Ashley, "you think you could help me draw that man?"

"Sure. I saw him real good," the girl said.

Miss Kennedy retrieved a sketch pad and pencils from the kitchen counter and returned to the table. The rest of the group leaned forward in anticipation. "If you don't mind," Miss Kennedy said as she flipped the sketch pad open to a blank page, "I'd like you all to wait in the other room. I can't work with a crowd."

"Okay," Bill said, motioning to Colleen, Myrtle, and Ashley's parents, "everyone out."

Colleen, Myrtle, and the parents retreated to the living room while Bill stayed behind.

"That includes you, Sheriff," Colleen heard the teacher say from the other room.

"Certainly," he said, forcing a smile, and crossed toward the living room.

Colleen bit her lip to keep from grinning. Bill was really having a tough time of it today. He entered the living room and passed her without making eye contact. The girl's parents huddled on the sofa, understandably anxious about the proceedings. Myrtle took a seat in a chair by the window and perused the art books on the coffee table. Bill positioned himself near the fireplace, directly across from the doorway and with an unobstructed view of the girl and her teacher at the table. Colleen contemplated joining him but decided against it. Better to give him his space. Instead, she leaned against the wall near the doorway, hoping to eavesdrop on the conversation in the kitchen.

"You remember how I taught you to start?" Colleen barely heard Miss Kennedy say.

"With the shape of the face?" the girl asked.

"Right. So was the shape like this?"

The room fell quiet. After that, the only words Colleen could make out were "round," "long nose," and an occasional "uh-huh." She saw from Bill's expression that he wasn't hearing any more than she was. At least he's seeing them, she thought. Now she wished she had taken her chances next to him.

Miss Kennedy and the girl worked in private in the kitchen,

whispering back and forth for the next fifteen minutes. In that time, Colleen had shifted her weight several times, Myrtle had become engrossed in an art history book, the father and mother had fought back tears, and Bill had remained a statue. Finally, they heard the sounds of chairs scraping on the floor and approaching footsteps.

Miss Kennedy and Ashley appeared in the doorway. "I think we're done," the teacher said. "She did a great job."

Ashley beamed and ran to her parents, who hugged her tight.

"So we're free to go?" the father asked Bill.

"If we need anything, we'll be in touch."

"I'll show you out," Miss Kennedy said and walked the parents to the door.

Myrtle joined Colleen and Bill in the doorway. "Now's the moment of truth," Myrtle said, inadvertently dropping her Uncle Mitch accent.

Colleen scowled at Myrtle and pointed to the teacher and girl saying good-bye. Myrtle quickly covered her mouth with her hand.

"Bye, Miss Kennedy," Ashley said from the street.

Miss Kennedy waved to the girl, then closed the front door. Colleen was eager to see the sketch. Soon they would know what the criminal who was plaguing their island looked like.

Bill held out his hand to receive the sketch. "Thank you for your help," he said as the teacher returned.

"I'm not done yet, Sheriff. It lacks the finishing touches."

"No offense, Miss Kennedy, but it doesn't need to be art."

"The man must have a context, an environment. For that I need to finish by the water."

"That's really not necessary," Bill said, losing his patience.

"You know your job, Sheriff, and I know mine. I won't be long." And with that the teacher was out the back door. "Oh, and Sheriff?" the group heard the teacher call from outside.

Bill started toward the back door.

"I work alone."

Bill stopped. Colleen averted her eyes. She didn't want to be the one who felt the brunt of his frustration, even though she had certainly contributed to it. He stood with his back to them.

"You want me to go out?" Colleen asked. "Maybe she'd feel differently with a woman."

"I don't like this," he said.

"I'm sure she'll be back in a moment," Myrtle said, trying to ease the tension. "You know artists . . . they're eccentric types."

"That may be," Bill said, facing them. "But I've had just about enough of eccentric types."

Ouch. The comment was directed at Colleen and Myrtle, and they both knew it.

"About Myrtle and me . . . we can explain," Colleen said, figuring now was as good a time as any to defend why they had deceived him.

"Nothing you say right now will help," he said, cutting her off.

"You don't need to make a federal case of it."

"That's exactly what it is. Or didn't you notice the agents excavating heroin from the dunes?"

Colleen's face flushed red. She could accept responsibility for hiding Myrtle but she wasn't going to take the blame for the drugs on the beach. "That's why I kept Myrtle hidden," she said. "Someone tried to kill her because of what she saw at the fireworks. If they're the same people involved with the heroin, you think they won't try again if they know she's still alive?"

"You should have told me," Bill said, his jaw set.

He was right. She should have told him. She was guilty as charged.

"It's my fault," Myrtle said. "I should have stayed in the chief's house like she instructed."

"*You* should have known better, Mrs. Crepe," Bill said.

The threesome fell into an uncomfortable silence, the kind of silence decent, otherwise reasonable people fall into when they are angry with one another. Deep down, they liked each other. They were part of the Corolla family. That's what made moments like this difficult. Genuine feelings of hatred would have been easier to deal with.

The floorboards creaked as Colleen shifted her weight. She checked the time. It had been a while since the teacher left. "Maybe we should go see how Miss Kennedy is doing," she said.

That was all Bill needed to hear. He spun on his heels and headed toward the back door, Colleen and Myrtle right behind him. He opened the screen door.

Colleen faced Myrtle. "Maybe you should stay out of sight."

"Right. Of course," Myrtle said. She let the screen door close in front of her as Colleen and Bill stepped from the back porch.

A path led through a small patch of pines toward Currituck Sound. Colleen and Bill made their way down the path in single file. They heard a rustling up ahead and stopped. Colleen peeked around Bill, expecting to see Miss Kennedy returning with her completed sketch. Instead, two wild horses emerged from the trees, crossed the path, and disappeared into the trees on the other side.

Colleen tapped on Bill's back to get him to move again. He jerked, startled.

"Sorry," she said. "Let's just hurry."

"My thoughts exactly."

The two picked up the pace and broke into a jog.

"Miss Kennedy?" Bill called as they reached the end of the path.

Colleen and Bill emerged from the grove of trees and came to a sudden stop. Miss Kennedy was slumped over the side of an Adirondack chair. Rumpled and burned sheets from the sketch pad whirled softly around her like falling cherry blossoms.

"Oh no," Colleen said and broke into a run.

They sprinted toward the teacher. Colleen slid to a stop, dropped to her knees, and gently lifted Miss Kennedy to an upright position. She tilted the woman's chin. Her neck had red, finger-shaped marks on it. Colleen searched for signs of inhaled or exhaled air, then put her ear to the woman's mouth. The teacher wasn't breathing. Colleen pressed two fingers to the woman's neck and checked for a pulse.

"Nothing," she said.

"Damn," Bill said, kicking the sand.

"Help me get her to the ground."

She and Bill swiftly eased the teacher to the sand. Colleen

pinched the woman's nose shut, gave two long, slow breaths, and checked for breathing and a pulse. "Call it in," she said to Bill as she positioned herself over the woman to perform CPR.

"Already on it," he said, pulling out his cell phone.

Come on, Miss Kennedy, Colleen prayed as she began CPR. She performed the fifteen-compression, two-breath cycle four times and felt again for a pulse. Still nothing. She heard Bill on the phone and could tell her guys were on their way. Sweat trickled down her temple. She repeated cycle after cycle but the teacher was nonresponsive. The woman was dead but she couldn't get herself to stop. She felt Bill's hand on her shoulder.

"She's gone," he said.

Colleen rolled to the side and rested her arms on her knees, exhausted. She checked her watch and noted the time of Miss Kennedy's death as the ambulance sirens wailed in the distance.

Chapter 14

"Chief McCabe . . . Sheriff Dorman . . . I'll speak with you now," said DEA Special Agent Javier Garcia after stepping into the hall of the Whalehead Beach Subdivision of the Currituck County Sheriff's Department. He signaled Colleen and Bill, then disappeared into the nearby office.

Colleen and Bill rose from the bench and made their way down the hall to Bill's office. Bill had agreed to allow the DEA team to use his office as a temporary headquarters, as it afforded them a table around which to gather as well as privacy from the other areas of the station. Even though Special Agent Garcia had treated Bill and Colleen with professional respect, Colleen felt like a scolded pupil sent to the principal's office. Garcia had kept them waiting in the hall for forty-five minutes and didn't smile when they entered.

"Close the door, please," Garcia said from the head of a large rectangular conference table.

Bill closed the door then joined Colleen at the table.

Agent Garcia rifled through a file of papers before looking up. "First off, I'd like to thank you for your cooperation in our investigation," the special agent said. "Sometimes local jurisdictions can feel as if we're stepping on their toes when we take over."

Colleen and Bill nodded but said nothing.

"And I'm sorry about the loss of Rosemary Kennedy. I understand she was a beloved teacher."

"Is the girl going to be safe?" Colleen asked, unable to contain the worry that had been building since the moment she had declared Miss Kennedy dead.

"That's why I wanted to speak with you. We're having trouble locating her family. It seems nobody's been home since they left the Kennedy residence and we can't pick up a cell phone signal."

"You think something happened to them?" Colleen asked.

"Right now we're more inclined to think they left town. You wouldn't happen to know if they were planning a trip or if they have family nearby?"

Colleen shook her head.

"I believe they have relatives in the Atlanta area. You may want to check with employers or at Ashley's school," Bill said.

"We're already on that," Garcia said. "The Kennedy homicide highlights the serious nature of this case. We'd like to find the girl before the man she saw finds her first. He's clearly dangerous."

Colleen flashed back to the night of the fireworks and the image of the man with the gun. Was he the man that the girl had seen on the beach? And was that man the murderer of the person found in Myrtle's house and the art teacher?

"It's unfortunate the sketch was destroyed," Garcia said.

Even though Agent Garcia's tone was friendly, she could tell by the way he fixed his eyes on them that his last statement was a reprimand.

"I never should have left Miss Kennedy alone," Bill said.

"Yes, we've covered that ground already. I'm interested in moving forward. We understand that you had a body wash up on the beach recently. A John Doe."

"Chief McCabe has a lead on a possible identity that I'd like to follow up on," Bill said.

"The John Doe may have been down from Pennsylvania for a week of fishing," she said. "I overheard guys at the Food Lion say his wife had been calling around because he hadn't been in touch with her. You think he's linked to Miss Kennedy's death?"

"I don't know. But I wouldn't assume he was here to fish. Seems more likely it was a drug deal gone bad."

Colleen was skeptical about Garcia's theory but kept her mouth shut. It didn't feel right to her that their John Doe came all the way down to the Outer Banks for drugs. Trafficking had been increasing in North Carolina, but it was almost exclusively inland and coming from the south, not the north. Even in the unlikely event that their John Doe was interested in buying drugs, there were plenty of stops between Pennsylvania and Corolla for that type of activity. Agent Garcia was clearly a bright man but it was obvious to Colleen from his fashionably coiffed hair, neatly pressed suit, and manicured fingernails that he wasn't an out-doorsman.

The phone in Bill's office rang. Bill reflexively moved to an-swer it, but it was Garcia who lifted the receiver. Colleen saw Bill's jaw clench; he was cooperating with the feds but he wasn't liking it.

"Garcia," the agent said into the phone. "Yeah, bring him down." Garcia hung up, crossed to the door, and opened it. "Let me know what you find out about your John Doe. And thanks again for the use of your office, Sheriff."

Colleen and Bill stood. They were being dismissed.

"Of course," Bill said, shaking Garcia's hand.

Colleen and Bill left the office and proceeded down the hall. As they neared the front entrance to the station, they heard screaming. They quickened their pace, turned the corner, and discovered Crazy Charlie being brought in in handcuffs by two DEA agents.

"Bring Mr. Nuckels down here," Garcia said.

Colleen marched toward Garcia. "Why are you bringing in Charlie?" she asked, knowing it was officially none of her business.

"We're covering all our bases," Garcia said, trying to move past her.

"You can't question him," she said, blocking Garcia.

"We can, Chief McCabe, and we will. Now, if you'll excuse me."

Colleen held her ground. "You don't understand," she said, lowering her voice so as not to be overheard by Charlie. "Charlie sees the world differently than you and I."

"Most suspects do," Garcia said and signaled his agents.

Charlie kicked and screamed as the agents hauled him down the hall. Colleen worried that if he gave them too much trouble he'd be physically forced into submission.

"Charlie, calm down," she said as the agents lugged Charlie by her.

Charlie panted and dragged his feet on the linoleum floor as the agents jerked him forward.

"This is ridiculous," Bill said to Garcia. "Charlie's family has lived on the island for generations. They're decent people."

"A lot of seemingly decent people have committed crimes. If what you're saying is true, Mr. Nuckels has nothing to worry about."

With that, Garcia and his agents disappeared down the hall and into Bill's office, Charlie squirming all the way. Charlie stole one last look at Colleen and Bill before Garcia closed the office door.

Colleen stared at Charlie's black scuff marks leading down the now empty hall. She and Bill had been shut out, literally. So much for the feds working with local law enforcement, she thought. If they really wanted to find out what was going on in Corolla, they were going to need her and Bill's help. Islanders would clam up if pushed too hard by nattily dressed mainlanders.

She checked to be sure she and Bill were alone. "Agent Garcia didn't ask about the fire or body at Myrtle's house," she said in a low voice.

"No," he said, avoiding eye contact.

"He must not think there's a connection between that death and Miss Kennedy's," she said, thinking aloud.

"Why would he?" Bill snapped. "Thanks to you and Myrtle, everyone thinks Myrtle was the one that died in that fire."

Colleen's face flushed red. What Bill didn't say was that thanks to her and Myrtle his career might be over. She was mortified. She had made him an accomplice in their deception and, in doing so, had put his job in jeopardy. Once the coroner identified the body, the jig would be up, Myrtle would be in danger, Bill's career would be over, and so would their friendship . . . unless she could figure out who was behind the recent crimes before the medical examiner's report came back and the feds discovered too much. Now, more than ever, she needed to uncover who was responsible for Corolla's unusual crime spree and she needed to do it fast.

Colleen and Bill stood in the hall alone, an awkward tension between them.

"I guess I should be getting to the station," she said.

"Sounds like a plan," Bill said.

"You heading out?"

"In a few minutes. Gotta talk to people at Joe's about the missing fisherman. You go on."

"I'll keep you posted if I find anything out."

"Good" was his terse response.

Colleen paused a moment, then walked away. So that's the

way it was going to be between them. Professional colleagues and nothing more. She had only herself to blame. She had violated a trust. It wouldn't matter that they had been friends for years. Working around Bill had taught her that he carefully weighed who earned his trust and who didn't. Once his trust had been given and broken it would be a long time before he gave it again, if he gave it again.

Colleen punched the door open and exited the building. She put on her sunglasses and stifled the urge to scream. She had to keep it together. What would the fellas at the station think if they saw their chief crying? She was the one they came to with family and relationship issues, not the other way around.

She slipped into her vehicle, thankful that earlier she had called Nellie to drive Myrtle and Sparky home from Miss Kennedy's house. Right now she needed to be alone. She started the engine and blasted the air-conditioning. She flipped down the visor mirror, dabbed tears from the inner corners of her eyes, and checked her face. Her nose was a little red but otherwise she looked fine. She closed the visor, threw the SUV into gear, and left the lot.

As she drove to the firehouse, she retrieved her cell phone and dialed home. She wanted to make sure Myrtle had made it back safely and that her cover hadn't been blown by spending too much time with Nellie. Ideally, Nellie would have dropped Myrtle and Sparky off and been on her way. But Colleen knew that that was too much to hope for. The two ladies were most likely sipping coffee and sharing stories in Colleen's kitchen.

The phone rang once, twice, three times and then the

answering machine picked up. Colleen disconnected and dialed again. She had instructed Myrtle that she would call, hang up, and call again if she wanted to speak with her. It was the signal they agreed to before Colleen and Bill left to talk to Special Agent Garcia. The phone rang again, once, twice, and then Myrtle answered.

"Hello," Myrtle said in her Mitch voice.

"Nellie still there?"

"How are you, Colleen?" Myrtle said, trying to play their call off as a mundane conversation.

"How are you?" she asked.

"Nell and I are getting on just fine. Aren't we, Nell?"

Colleen heard Nellie answer in the affirmative in the background.

"You mind if I go into the other room and talk to my niece?" she heard Myrtle ask Nellie.

Colleen's eyebrows furrowed. Something was up. She pulled onto the shoulder. She didn't want to be driving in case it was bad news.

"You there?" Myrtle asked in her own voice after a pause.

"What's up?" Colleen asked, concerned.

"I've been waiting for your call. Did everything go okay with the DEA?"

"I'm not sure I'd use that word to describe how things went."

"Then you're not going to like what I've got to tell you," Myrtle said in a hushed tone.

Colleen had a disguised former teacher at her house, a dead body washed up on the beach, a burned body at the medical examiner's office, a missing little girl, heroin buried in the dunes, a mysterious man with a gun, and a dead art teacher. What more could Myrtle add to the list?

"Things happened so fast at Miss Kennedy's house I didn't have time to tell you."

"What is it?" Colleen asked with an edge. She was starting to panic and Myrtle drawing things out wasn't helping.

"While you and Sheriff Dorman were with poor Miss Kennedy I was looking out her front window. I saw a car in front of her house, just sitting there with the engine running."

"What kind of car?"

"I don't know. Four-door. New, I guess. It was sort of a gray or silver color."

Colleen's heart skipped a beat. She broke into a cold sweat. A charcoal-colored sedan had been parked near the house where Myrtle and the girl had been hidden.

"Would you say the car was charcoal in color?" she asked, trying to remain calm.

"I guess. Yeah, I guess I'd say it was dark gray."

"Myrtle, tell me you saw the driver."

"The car drove away before I could," Myrtle said, slipping back into her Uncle Mitch voice.

Colleen heard Nellie in the background asking if everything was okay. Myrtle would have to get off the phone or arouse Nellie's suspicion. "Thanks for the information," she said. "I'll call you later."

"Good talking to you," Myrtle said and then the connection went dead.

Colleen sighed. Myrtle would have to be on her own for a while longer. She hoped her acting skills were as good as she said they were. She wasn't sure how Nellie would take the deception if she discovered that Mitch was really Myrtle. Bill certainly hadn't liked it.

Colleen merged into traffic. She was running out of time. Sooner or later Myrtle would be found out, and once that happened her former teacher would be in danger again. And she didn't even want to dwell on what might have happened to Ashley and her family. Her gut told her they were okay, safely tucked away somewhere, but she had also thought the art teacher was safe at her own home. She decided to take a detour before going to the station. She needed to find the charcoal-colored sedan and its driver. She had a feeling both were still on the island and that was the reason why the coroner was suddenly getting a lot of business. Colleen went north, back to where she had first spotted the sedan near the partially constructed beach house. She didn't think it likely the car would be there, but it was the only place she knew to look.

As she sped up Route 12, Colleen wondered how the killer had known the girl was at Miss Kennedy's house. The obvious answer was that he had followed them. If that were true, then he must have known where the girl and Myrtle had been hidden. But she and Myrtle had thoroughly checked the property before stashing the girl there. They hadn't seen anyone near the house and the empty sedan had been parked at least fifty yards away. She was certain the site had been deserted. Still, something nagged at her.

She strained her memory, trying to recall every detail of the events at the beach house. Was there a shadow she had missed lurking in a corner? The smell of someone's cologne or sweat? Colleen's seat squeaked underneath her as she bounced over a pothole. Suddenly, her mind clicked. The squeaking and groaning floorboards! How could she have been so stupid? She had blamed the wind for its cause but someone must have been moving around above them inside the house and overheard everything they had said! No wonder Miss Kennedy's killer knew where to find the girl. From the elevated vantage point he probably had a view not only of Bill's vehicle driving away but the DEA agents digging up the heroin.

Colleen felt like an idiot. She had forgotten to look up. She recalled being on a high school field trip to Washington, D.C., and one of the teachers telling the group to "turn their eyes to the heavens." He had said that thousands of people walked by the buildings every day and never noticed the brilliant work artisans had done on the façades. Much of the day had been spent discovering carved gargoyles and eagles and other creatures hovering above them. From then on, she was aware of the underbelly of bird's nests, the way snow fell from directly above, and the frequency of shooting stars. She had made it a habit to observe what was above her . . . except today.

Colleen drew near the beach house. She could already see that the sedan wasn't there, but she stopped at the house anyway. She examined the partially finished second floor. From there the killer most certainly could have seen and heard everything.

As she studied the house, something in the sky caught her eye. She removed her sunglasses, wound down her window, and squinted into the sun. A light breeze carried smoke over the tops of the houses and out to sea. Colleen sniffed the air and frowned. Pinky was up to his old tricks.

Chapter 15

"You know Pinky," Colleen said to Jimmy Bartlett over her cell phone as she drove toward the Island Sands development. "Where there's smoke, there's fire."

"That's what I'm worried about," Jimmy said in a stern tone. "You call if it's more than Mr. Salvatore's debris that's on fire."

Colleen grinned. One thing she could count on was Jimmy turning into a big brother when she had to visit Pinky. It didn't matter that she was Jimmy's boss. "If Sheriff Dorman comes looking for me, let him know where I am," she said and hung up.

Colleen thumped the steering wheel. Damn. Why did she leave that message for Bill with Jimmy? If Bill wanted to share information about the missing fisherman he would simply call her. Did she really think Bill was more likely to stop by the station than pick up the phone? Of course not. If she was being completely honest with herself she knew leaving the message with Jimmy almost guaranteed Jimmy would call Bill and tell him about her trip to see Pinky. And when Bill heard about the visit, maybe, just maybe, he'd worry about her a little. Leaving the message was a feeble attempt to get Bill's attention. Pathetic, she thought.

Colleen rounded the final bend that led into Island Sands. She wound through the estate community and found the source of the smoke. Pinky's workers must have seen her vehicle approaching because they were already busy hosing down the burning debris. Colleen swung her vehicle in a wide circle around them. None of the workers made eye contact with her. She slowed to watch the last flames fizzle out, then continued to Pinky's trailer. Today would not be a good day for Antonio Salvatore.

When she arrived at Pinky's glorified double-wide trailer with its Vegas-style faux New York–skyline façade, the sight of Little Bobby's motorcycle in the parking lot made her forget her mental preparations for Pinky's tongue lashing. What was Little Bobby doing here? She parked in the shade behind a thicket of carefully landscaped trees and shrubs and exited her vehicle. The door to Pinky's trailer opened. She quietly closed her SUV door and ducked behind the vegetation.

"When you get the title changed let me know and I'll draw up the papers," Pinky said, descending the steps with Little Bobby.

"The sooner we can get this done the better," Little Bobby said.

Colleen heard movement in the trees behind her and froze. Was it the man with the gun? Had Pinky laid a trap for her by starting the fire? Did he have someone waiting to attack her? She heard the familiar sounds of snorting and chewing. She peeked over her shoulder, saw a horse grazing nearby, and sighed with relief.

"Thanks for coming by, Mr. Crepe," Pinky said, capturing her attention.

Little Bobby mounted his motorcycle, donned his helmet, revved the engine, and raced from the property. When he was gone, Pinky climbed the stairs and retreated inside the trailer.

Colleen was so stunned by the interaction between Pinky and Little Bobby that she almost forgot the reason for her visit. Suddenly, her goal had changed from shutting Pinky down for burning debris to finding out what deal he had conned Little Bobby into accepting. A different goal meant she'd have to employ different tactics. She'd still fine Pinky for the debris—that, he would expect—but she couldn't give him too much trouble if she was going to get information from him. She took a deep breath and cut across the steamy parking lot. This was going to require all the charm she could muster.

Colleen climbed the trailer steps and was about to knock when the door opened wide. "Chief McCabe, how lovely to see you," Pinky greeted her.

He stepped aside and motioned for her to go in. Frank Sinatra sang "I Get a Kick Out of You" softly over the speakers. She eyed Pinky in her peripheral vision as she entered. Had he known she was out in the parking lot all along? She'd have to stay on her toes. Despite his apparent interest in her, Pinky wasn't easily manipulated.

"May I get you some champagne?" he asked, crossing to a small bar.

"What's the celebration?"

"You don't need to celebrate to have champagne," he said with a smile, and extracted a chilled bottle from an ice bucket that had been standing at the ready on the kitchen counter.

Colleen surveyed the interior of Pinky's trailer. It never ceased to amaze her how clean and contemporary it was, like something out of a high-end interior design magazine. When she had visited friends who lived in the trailer park, the insides of their double-wide homes never looked like this.

Pinky poured two glasses of champagne. Colleen had no intention of drinking hers but she accepted the champagne and played along. Maybe she could get Pinky a little tipsy.

"So what brings you to my neck of the island?" he asked.

She resisted the urge to take a sip. The glass felt cool in her hand and the bubbles looked refreshingly tempting. "It's about the debris," she said.

"It's always about the debris," Pinky said, tasted his drink, and let out a satisfied sigh. "You haven't tried your champagne. I don't break out the good stuff for just anyone, Chief McCabe."

Colleen reluctantly took a sip. She knew if she didn't she'd never find out what Pinky and Little Bobby had been discussing and the visit would end like all visits with Pinky—her handing him a fine and him clinging to her hand a little too long as he shook it to say good-bye. "Delicious," she said. The champagne really was delicious. If Colleen didn't have to work and it was Bill instead of Pinky, she definitely could have been persuaded into indulging in a glass or two.

"Shall we?" he said with a wink and indicated the living room area of the trailer.

Colleen eyed the sectional leather furniture. No matter where she sat, Pinky could sit next to her. She forced a smile, then chose a spot in the middle of the longer section of the sofa. Sitting in the middle allowed her plenty of room to get away if he tried to make an amorous advance. Surprisingly, Pinky chose a seat adjacent to hers. He leaned back into the pillows, put his glass up to one eye, and gazed at her through the champagne.

"What are you doing?" she asked, unsure what to make of this.

"Trying to see what you'd look like surrounded by bubbles," he said.

Colleen squirmed and set her champagne on the glass-and-chrome coffee table. She resisted the urge to clobber Pinky. "Mr. Salvatore, how long are we going to play this little game?" she asked.

"What game is that?" he asked, leaning forward with interest.

"The one where you burn debris and I fine you. Don't you think it's getting old?"

"Do you have something new in mind?"

She fought back a shudder. The thought of her and Pinky was too bizarre. They were from two different worlds. No matter how attractive, charming, or successful other women found

Pinky, he was another species to Colleen. Maybe that's what he liked about her. Perhaps he found her exotic, as crazy as that seemed.

"How about you stop burning the debris? That would be new," she said, wanting to keep the conversation professional.

He sighed with disappointment and sat back. "I thought you said you were tired of the old game."

You want a new game, Pinky, I'll give you one, she thought. "Okay then. How about we talk about the pyrotechnics company and Mrs. Crepe's house exploding."

Pinky smirked. "Now that *is* a new game. One I believe you started at Mrs. Crepe's memorial service."

"Well?" she asked.

Pinky rose, crossed to the kitchen, and poured himself another glass of champagne. "As I told you before, I'm not in the business of acquiring property through illegal means," he said and rested against the counter.

"Then what was Bobby Crepe doing here earlier?"

Pinky stared at Colleen a long moment. She found herself holding her breath. She had never known him to be at a loss for words.

"I don't discuss business deals with outside parties," he finally said.

"But you are doing business with Bobby Crepe."

"Yes."

How dare Pinky manipulate Bobby when he was still grieving for his not-so-dead mother! She rose from the sofa in a burst of anger. "How could you!"

He raised his eyebrows in surprise. "How could I what?"

"How could you prey on Bobby when he just lost his mother? It's despicable."

Pinky put down his champagne glass. "Is that what you think of me?"

Colleen studied him. He appeared to be genuinely hurt. A hint of doubt surfaced in her mind but she pushed it down. Pinky deliberately crossed to her. She stiffened, unsure whether he wanted to hit or kiss her. She stood ready to defend herself. Pinky stepped into her personal space.

"You seem to be operating under a misconception," he said. "Bobby Crepe approached me about selling the family property, not the other way around. You may not believe it, but I respect family. I'd never approach a man who was grieving over the loss of his mother."

"But you're not opposed to him approaching you," Colleen said, her anger subsiding as her mind whirled about Bobby selling Myrtle's house.

"Buying and selling property is how I make my living. I won't apologize for acquiring a desirable piece of real estate that, to be quite honest, his mother refused to sell to me."

"And you have no knowledge of anyone who might do something, let's say illegal, to speed that process along?"

Pinky clenched his jaw. "No."

She stared him straight in the eyes. He was either a really good liar or he was telling the truth. Despite his apparent discomfort with her last question, her gut told her he was being honest with her. Her face flushed anew, this time from embarrassment. She had insulted the chief business benefactor to the Corolla Fire and Rescue's SEAL Kids program. If he asked her out now, she'd say yes and wear a dress to boot.

"I'm sorry," she said. "I didn't mean to imply . . ." She found herself unable to finish her sentence.

"Yes, you did," he said, moving away to the kitchen. "And I accept your apology."

Colleen looked at him wide-eyed.

"Don't look so surprised, Chief McCabe. I've been accused of far worse. I admire the passion you showed in confronting what you perceived as a wrong. Most people wouldn't do that, especially with me."

"I guess I'm not like most people," she said with a weak smile.

"No, you're not." Pinky admired her for a moment, then removed a pen from his pocket. "So, shall we get to what brought you here?"

Colleen's brows furrowed with uncertainty.

"I believe there's the business of paying a fine," he said, uncapping his fountain pen.

Oh yes, the fine. She pulled a pad from her back pocket. They may be from different planets, but she had to respect Pinky's moral code. Colleen wrote out the fine; Pinky signed it; she handed him his copy; and he walked her to the door. When she stepped onto the trailer's landing, he touched her arm.

"Thank you," he said.

"For what?" she asked.

"An interesting visit. It's the one thing I can count on from you, Chief McCabe," he said and winked.

Colleen grinned, put on her sunglasses, and descended the stairs. It's the one thing I can count on from you, too, Antonio Salvatore, she thought, and crossed the lot to her SUV.

Chapter 16

The news of Little Bobby selling the Crepe property to Pinky Salvatore whirled in Colleen's head. It had only been a little over two weeks since Myrtle's "death." If Bobby was grieving for his mother, buying a motorcycle and selling the family home was an unusual way of showing it. She wondered how Bobby had managed to get the ball rolling on the sale of the house so swiftly. Changing a property title wasn't necessarily an easy or quick thing.

When Colleen was in her mid-twenties, she and her mother had inherited a condominium from an aunt in Tampa, Florida. Since neither of them wanted to move to a retirement community, they had decided to sell the condo. Unfortunately, because of the way the will had been written, the property had had to go through probate. It took eighteen months before the circuit court clerk for Pinellas County signed off on the estate and freed them to put the condo on the market. Colleen hoped Myrtle's will was drawn up in a similar fashion so that the sale of the house would be delayed. If not, Myrtle might lose her home. If Myrtle lost her home, she'd end up living with Colleen indefinitely—something Colleen didn't relish.

She felt obligated to tell Myrtle about what she had learned about Bobby's negotiations with Pinky but was worried about how Myrtle would react to the news. Myrtle would certainly want to confront her son and the only way she could do that would be by coming out of hiding. However, doing that would put Myrtle in danger. Colleen wished she could keep the information about Bobby selling the house to herself, but keeping secrets had already done enough damage.

She checked her watch. She had sufficient time to swing by her house and look in on Myrtle before heading to the station. With any luck, Nellie would be gone and she and Myrtle could speak freely. If not, she'd have to save the house sale conversation for later.

She drove the short distance up Ocean Trail to the turnoff for her property. She was surprised to see Bill's SUV parked in front of her house. She pulled in next to Bill and threw her SUV into park. She hopped out and was startled when the door to his car suddenly swung open.

"Bill," she said with a gasp. "What are you doing here?"

"I was just, um, checking . . ." he said.

Bill paced between their vehicles. She walked around her car to eliminate the barrier between them. "Checking what?"

"I called your cell. Antonio Salvatore answered."

Colleen searched her pockets. No phone. "It must have fallen out in his trailer."

"I suppose you'll have to go back to get it then?" Bill asked rather forcefully.

"I suppose."

Colleen studied Bill as he alternately put his hands in and took them out of his pockets. His mood seemed a combination of irritation and anxiety. Normally, she'd ask him what was on his mind but, given their recent conflict, didn't feel he'd offer her an explanation. At least they were talking, even if somewhat awkwardly.

"With everything that's been going on lately, I wanted to make sure things were okay," he said, regaining his composure and assuming a professional tone.

Somewhere in the back of Colleen's mind she hoped that Bill had driven to her house because he was concerned about her. Instead, he was just doing his job. "Would you like to come inside?" she asked, hiding her disappointment. "You can check on Myrtle and be on your way."

Bill nodded and indicated she should lead. Colleen walked up the steps and opened the front door. "Hello?" she called as they entered.

Colleen heard the rapid click of nails on hardwood. Seconds later, Sparky bounded around the corner, his tail wagging. "Hey there," she said and rubbed the dog's side.

Bill closed the door behind them.

"Hello?" Myrtle said from inside the bathroom in her normal, non-Mitch speaking voice.

"It's just me and Sheriff Dorman, Myrtle."

The bathroom door opened and Myrtle emerged. She was no longer wearing the mustache but was still dressed in Colleen's father's clothes. "I know who blew up my house," she said, storming toward them.

Colleen and Bill exchanged looks of surprise. "Who?" they asked in unison.

"Nellie Byrd!"

"Oh, come on," Colleen said.

"I'm telling you, she did it," Myrtle said in a huff.

"Why don't we take a seat at the kitchen table," Colleen said.

"I don't need to sit."

"It's been a long morning. Indulge me."

"It sounds like a good idea, Mrs. Crepe," Bill said.

"Fine."

Figures she'd listen when Bill asked her, Colleen thought. After all she and Myrtle had been through, Myrtle still deferred to the authority of a man.

"Can I get anyone something to drink?" she asked as the group entered the kitchen.

"Nothing for me," Bill said, standing at the head of the table near the window.

"I'll take a whiskey sour," Myrtle said.

"You'll have water."

"If that's my only option," Myrtle said and took a seat at the table with a dramatic sweep.

"Why do you think Nellie set your house on fire?" Bill asked as Colleen filled the glasses.

"She told me Colleen gave her the Society documents this week."

"I did," Colleen said, bringing three glasses to the table.

"Those documents belong with me. I'm the president."

"Not as long as you're dead, you're not," she said.

Even though Bill had declined a beverage, he took one of the glasses and gulped down the water. Colleen suppressed a satisfied smile. Smokey appeared from around the corner and jumped into Myrtle's lap.

"Smokey, no," she said, reaching for the cat.

Myrtle moved her arm protectively around the Siamese. "It's okay."

"She's not allowed up like that at the table, Myrtle."

"She likes it," Myrtle said, squeezing the cat and rubbing her cheek.

To Colleen's annoyance Smokey curled into Myrtle's lap and purred loudly with smug satisfaction. She stared at the cat in defeat. It was going to take weeks after Myrtle left to retrain the stubborn Siamese.

"Could we forget about the cat?" Bill asked with irritation.

Colleen and Myrtle looked at him with surprise.

"Mrs. Crepe, I don't see how you can draw the conclusion that Nellie Byrd burned your house down just to get possession of the Society's documents."

"So you aren't going to arrest her?"

"This seems like more of a personal than a police matter."

"Besides," Colleen said, "I thought you two were getting along."

"We were . . . until Mitch came along. I think she likes him better than me."

"You *are* Mitch."

"Nellie doesn't know that."

Bill shook his head.

"Let's suppose, for the sake of argument, that Nellie likes you as Mitch better than she likes you as you," Colleen said, wanting to get Myrtle back on track. "What does that have to do with your house fire?"

"Nellie told Mitch that she resented how I sometimes excluded her from Society decisions. I didn't exclude her. I merely filtered what she did or didn't need to know."

"That doesn't make her an arsonist," Bill said.

"I'm telling you she did it!" Myrtle said, startling Smokey off her lap and sending her scurrying from the room.

"If the documents were so important to her, why would she leave them behind in your house to burn in the fire?" Colleen asked, rising from her chair. "It doesn't make any sense."

"She was obviously willing to sacrifice the documents if it meant getting rid of me."

Colleen was losing her patience. "You honestly believe Nellie is capable of arson and murder?"

"Who else could it be?"

"What about Bobby?" she asked, her voice rising in frustration. The second she blurted it out she wished she could take it back. This wasn't how she had planned on breaking the news to Myrtle.

"What do you mean—what about Bobby?" Myrtle asked.

Myrtle and Bill waited. She was going to have to tell them about Bobby's sale of the Crepe family residence. There was no way around it. "Bobby is selling your house."

"Over my dead body," Myrtle said, springing from her seat.

"Exactly," Colleen said, pointedly.

Myrtle gaped at Colleen in stunned silence, then began pacing the kitchen. Sparky followed her every move, thinking he was going to get a treat.

"How do you know this?" Bill asked.

"Pinky Salvatore told me."

"And you believe that gangster?" he asked, his face flushing red.

"Yes, I do."

"Really, Colleen!" Myrtle said in disbelief.

"Why would Mr. Salvatore share business information with *you*?" Bill asked, his anger boiling to the surface.

"I don't know," Colleen said, irritated at his tone. "Maybe because I asked."

"Right," he said under his breath.

"You were with that hoodlum?"

"I asked him a question and he gave me an answer. That's more than I can say for our conversations lately," Colleen said to Bill, ignoring Myrtle's question.

"Excuse me if I've been a little put off after finding out Myrtle survived the fire and you knew about it."

"Aaaaah!" Myrtle roared.

Colleen and Bill jumped. Sparky hastily retreated to his bed in the living room.

"Enough," Myrtle said, her breathing heavy. "I'm too old for this."

The room fell silent. Nobody moved. Colleen glanced at Bill and Myrtle. This was not good. If they were going to ascertain who killed Jane Doe and burned Myrtle's house, strangled the art teacher, buried the heroin on the beach, and also learn the identity of the John Doe that had washed ashore, they were going to have to work together. That meant setting aside differences and hurt feelings—at least until after the crimes were solved.

"I'm sorry, Myrtle," she said, taking the first step. "I didn't mean to tell you about Bobby this way. I sincerely hope he didn't set the fire but in light of what I learned from Pinky, we have to consider the possibility."

"What about what I learned? Doesn't that make Nellie a suspect, too?"

"I suppose so," she said, not wanting to resume arguing. "So we've got Bobby and Nellie as possible suspects in the arson and Jane Doe death. And let's not forget the man with the gun who we saw at the fireworks."

"What man with a gun?" Bill asked.

"Maybe he's the drug dealer that killed Miss Kennedy," Myrtle said to Colleen.

"Excuse me," Bill tried again. "What man with a gun?"

"It's a possibility," Colleen said to Myrtle.

"Hey!" he said, raising his voice and silencing the women. "What man with a gun?"

Myrtle pointed at Colleen, indicating she should tell Bill. Thanks a lot, Colleen thought.

"The night of the fireworks Myrtle and I saw a man with a gun lurking near the Lighthouse. Myrtle thinks she saw some other men with guns, too . . . before that."

Bill shook his head in disgust. "And why haven't you told me about this until now?"

"I forgot?" she said, sheepish.

Bill scowled at them. Colleen and Myrtle squirmed.

"Anything else you two *forgot* to tell me?"

"No," they said together.

He studied them and sighed. "Okay."

Silence filled the room. Myrtle fidgeted in her chair. Bill unconsciously tapped his thigh.

Colleen took a deep breath. "So," she said, gingerly, "where were we?"

"List of suspects, I believe," Myrtle said.

Colleen glanced at Bill. "Did you find anything out at Joe's?"

Bill folded his arms and stared at her. "Haven't you forgotten someone else who might have burned Myrtle's house? Someone who has a history of burning things."

He meant Pinky Salvatore. Colleen felt strongly that Pinky hadn't been involved, but if they were going to include Nellie Byrd on the suspects list, they'd have to include Salvatore. "You're talking about Pinky."

"Of course," Myrtle said. "He's been trying to get his hands on my property for years."

"That's not the only thing he's been trying to get his hands on," Bill said under his breath.

Myrtle looked at Bill, puzzled, but Colleen knew what he

meant. As absurd as it seemed to her, he was jealous of the time she had spent with the real estate developer. In order to convince him she wasn't romantically interested in Pinky, she'd have to agree to add Pinky's name to the growing list of suspects. "Very well. Pinky's on the list, too," Colleen said without conviction.

Bill nodded, satisfied.

"So what did the folks at Joe's say about the missing fisherman?" she asked, wanting to get off the topic of Pinky.

"What missing fisherman?" Myrtle asked.

Colleen held her tongue. She'd let Bill determine what to tell Myrtle. He hesitated. *He's trying to decide if he can trust us,* she thought, and hoped Bill wouldn't hold it against them that they hadn't told him about the man with the gun.

"Turns out a Pennsylvania man who came down to fish has gone missing," he finally said. "We're trying to figure out if a body that washed up on the beach a short time ago is this man."

"How come I didn't hear about this on the news?"

"We've managed to keep it out of the press."

"So did you get a name?" Colleen asked, relieved that they were back to collaborating.

"Frank Bremer. His wife signed a release for the dental records. Images should be e-mailed by today, tomorrow at the latest."

"That'll help confirm who he is but not what happened to him, why it happened, or if it's connected to anything else that's been going on," Colleen said.

"We won't know how he died until the coroner's report, but at least it's a start."

Bill's cell phone rang. He checked the number. "It's the office," he said. "Hey, Rodney, what's up?"

Colleen and Myrtle watched and waited.

"Really? Are you sure? Did he say why?" Bill listened as Rodney spoke on the other end.

Colleen could see by his reaction that he had received some troubling news. She couldn't imagine what it could be—there had been so much of it lately.

"Thanks for calling," he said and hung up.

"Is everything okay?" she asked.

Bill stood with his hands on his hips. "Charlie confessed to setting fire to Myrtle's house and, as a result, killing our Jane Doe."

"Charlie Nuckels?" Myrtle asked, shocked.

"I don't believe it," Colleen said.

"Neither do I. But he signed a confession and his boot prints match those found outside the house."

"All that means is that he was at Myrtle's. We already knew that."

"Why would he confess to something he didn't do?" Myrtle asked.

"There's more. Apparently, he also confessed to the heroin."

"This is ridiculous," Colleen said with growing irritation. "He probably didn't even know what he was confessing to. You know Charlie."

"Charlie's a gentle giant," Myrtle said sadly.

"ATF has been called in. Looks like we're gonna have more feds in town. I think they're trying to link Charlie to Miss Kennedy's homicide as well."

How could Agent Garcia possibly think Crazy Charlie committed all those crimes? Maybe she had given the special agent more credit than he deserved. Colleen could just imagine the interrogation scenario in Bill's office. The agents had probably enticed Charlie to confess with incentives such as cola and ice cream. Knowing Charlie as she did, he would have told them anything if it meant being the center of attention. But sitting in an interrogation room was a picnic compared to federal prison. She shuddered to think what jail might do to him. Despite being a large, imposing man, Charlie had a fragility to him. If confined to a cell, Crazy Charlie just might earn his nickname.

"Bill, we've got to do something," she said, deeply concerned about Charlie's welfare.

"Not much we can do."

"But we must. We may not have the same opinion about who committed the arson, but we all know it wasn't Charlie."

"Agreed," Myrtle said.

"We can't interfere with a federal investigation," Bill said.

He had a point. It was one thing getting involved in Bill's local cases; it was another getting involved with the Justice Department. Maybe there was a loophole. "But there's nothing wrong with talking to our suspects in a general sense, is there?"

"No," he said. "Okay. How about Myrtle contacts Nellie, you contact Bobby, and I contact Salvatore."

Colleen didn't like the idea of Bill visiting Pinky. "I left the phone at Pinky's trailer. If we don't want to arouse suspicion, it makes more sense for me to go."

Bill clenched his jaw. She knew he wasn't happy with the idea of her being alone with Pinky again, particularly since he obviously believed the developer capable of arson and murder.

"I hate to say it, Sheriff, but Colleen's right," Myrtle said. "For some reason, that mobster likes her."

"Thanks," Colleen said. "I think."

"Then at least let me follow you, in case something happens."

"I think Mr. Salvatore must have surveillance in his development. He and his men always seem to know when I'm coming. If that's the case, he'll know something's up as soon as he sees your vehicle. I'm sorry, Bill, but I've got to go alone."

Colleen knew her argument made sense. She also knew that there was good reason for Bill's concern. Of all the persons on their list, Pinky seemed the most capable, if not the most probable in her mind, of committing a crime.

"Fine," he said. "But as soon as you pick up your phone I want you to call me. In the meantime, Myrtle, I'll drop you at Nell's shop. You'll need to be there as Mitch. Pretend like you're buying lures or something. I'll pay a visit to your son. He seems to be hanging out at Joe's a lot lately."

"Give me a minute to put on my mustache," Myrtle said and left the room.

Colleen picked up the water glasses and placed them in the sink.

"You sure you're going to be okay?" Bill asked.

"If I can handle a station full of men, I can handle Antonio Salvatore," she said, trying to put him at ease.

Frankly, she was a little nervous about calling on Pinky. Now that he was a suspect on their list, doubts about Pinky's innocence were creeping in. Had she been wrong to be so cavalier about him? What if there was a dark side to Pinky? And what exactly was she going to say to him when she got there? Telling him that she was there to pick up her cell phone would seem as if she had planted the phone as an excuse to come back and visit him. What if he took it as a romantic gesture?

"Shall we?" Myrtle asked, rejoining them in full disguise.

Colleen, Bill, and Myrtle made their way outside. Sparky followed and whimpered for Colleen to take him with her.

"Stay," she said. If she was going to be in any type of danger, she didn't want Sparky with her.

The Border collie flopped down on the porch with a sigh. Bill helped Myrtle into his vehicle as Colleen opened the door to her SUV.

"Colleen?" he said.

She glanced at Bill over the roof.

"Call me as soon as you get your phone."

Colleen saluted. Bill smiled at her gesture but she could tell he was worried. Truth be told, she was a little worried, too.

Chapter 17

As soon as Colleen cruised into the deserted lot in front of Pinky's trailer she sensed something was amiss. It was close to ninety-five degrees and yet the front door stood wide open. She had never known him to leave his door ajar. She had learned over the course of her multiple visits that this was for three reasons: 1) Pinky suffered from allergies for which he received shots every other week. 2) He was the king of clean and would never invite dirt into his spotless trailer. And 3) Despite his tendency toward excess in the design of his properties, Pinky was not generally wasteful. The open door was definitely unusual. Maybe she should have brought Bill along after all.

Colleen slowed and parked. She searched the lot for any signs of activity or trouble. A swallow swooped over the windshield and landed on the branch of a nearby pine. She cut the engine, stepped from her vehicle, and eyed her surroundings as she cautiously approached the trailer. The cool sounds of Frank Sinatra crooning "That's Life" spilled from the office on the draft of seventy-degree conditioned air. She reached the landing and peered in through the door.

"Mr. Salvatore?" she said, not wanting to startle him if he was inside.

Sinatra responded over the speakers but nothing from Pinky. She took a step over the threshold, leaned into the opening, and peeked around the door. She scanned the room and was alarmed to find it littered with broken glass from the coffee table.

"Pinky?" she said and entered. The carpet was damp where champagne had spilled from an overturned bottle and the paintings on one wall were askew. She moved toward the phone in the kitchen to call for help and discovered Pinky unconscious on the floor. Not again, Colleen thought, and rushed to the man's side. She knelt next to him and listened. She heard the gentle inhalation and exhalation of air and felt his warm breath on her ear. She put her fingers to his neck, found a pulse, and sighed with relief. Pinky had been knocked down but not permanently out.

"That's Life" faded and "Someone to Watch Over Me"—the next song on the playlist—blared from the speakers. Colleen stood, searched for the controls for the stereo system, and turned the sound down. She returned to Pinky. "Mr. Salvatore? It's Chief McCabe," she said, gently patting his hand.

Pinky's breathing deepened and his eyes blinked open.

"Hello," she said quietly, not wanting to frighten him in case he was disoriented.

Pinky groaned as he struggled to sit up. She helped him lean against the back of the bar. "Are you okay?"

"I am now that you're here, my funny valentine."

Colleen couldn't help but smile. Even in a semiconscious state he was amorous. "Let's get you up," she said and swung her arm behind Pinky's back and under his arms.

While helping Pinky to his feet and the sofa, Colleen noticed swelling on the side of his head. She eased him down and added pillows to support his back.

"To what do I owe the pleasure of your visit?" he asked, gingerly touching the bump.

"I left my cell phone here."

"It's on the counter," he said, motioning toward the kitchen.

She spotted her phone on the counter, then turned to examine Pinky. "Mind telling me what happened?"

"My nephew's what happened," he said, placing another pillow behind his back. "Max was such a sweet kid—it's how he got the nickname Sweet Boy—but ever since my sister divorced his father he's had a tough go of it."

Colleen's brows furrowed. Why did that name sound familiar? "He's been living with you?" she asked.

Pinky nodded and winced. "My sister shipped him down. I think that hurt him—being sent away. She thinks he needs a man in his life since his father has apparently started a new one with a new family."

"How come I haven't seen him here at the trailer with you?"

"I suggested he work with me. He says I'm boring."

Colleen cocked her head. One thing Pinky wasn't was boring.

She rose and moved to the kitchen. "Why would he attack you?" she asked, slipping her phone into her pocket. She grabbed a towel from a hook on the wall and ran it under water.

"I told him to make himself useful."

"That's it?"

Pinky shrugged. "He's got too much Cascio and not enough Salvatore blood in him. The Cascios have hot tempers. Me, I'm more of a lover than a fighter."

You can say that again, Colleen thought. She filled the damp towel with ice and returned to Pinky. "Put this on that bump until my guys get here."

"I'm fine."

"I'm going to make sure of that." She retrieved her phone and speed-dialed the station.

Jimmy answered on the first ring. "Everything okay?" he asked with concern.

"Could you send the EMT unit over to Antonio Salvatore's trailer? I found him unconscious. He seems fairly lucid now but has a contusion on his head and needs to be checked out."

"Got it," Jimmy said and hung up.

"Any idea where your nephew is now?" she asked, repositioning where Pinky held the ice.

"Probably wrecking the car I gave him. You should see it. Has a beautiful custom charcoal-gray paint job."

Her eyes widened. It was the car at the beach house. "Did you say charcoal gray?"

"Love that color. Reminds me of the Chrysler Building's art deco elevators I used to ride in as a kid."

"Care to tell me what you two were fighting about?"

"Let's just say he and I have different ideas about the type of business the family should be in."

Colleen recalled the shadowy gunman from the Lighthouse. Could that have been Pinky's nephew, Max "Sweet Boy" Cascio? And could he be the same man who had burned down Myrtle's house with Jane Doe inside, buried the heroin, and killed Miss Kennedy? If so, Pinky was lucky to get away with just a bump on the head. She wondered how much Pinky knew about what his nephew had been up to on the island and if he had been covering anything up.

She heard the engine of a vehicle in the lot. "That must be the EMTs," she said, jumping from the sofa and hurrying toward the door.

She swung the front door open and froze. Idling in the lot was the charcoal-colored sedan. "Hey!" she said, stepping outside.

The sedan engine revved and the car zoomed from the parking lot. Colleen watched it disappear, then ran back inside. "Stay put and lock the door," she said to Pinky before leaving and slamming the door closed behind her.

She leapt down the steps of the trailer and dashed to her SUV. She started the engine, flipped on the emergency lights, and peeled out of the lot. If it's a chase Pinky's nephew wanted, it was a chase he was going to get. In her early twenties, Colleen had been known for her lead foot and skill behind the wheel. She had even won a couple of amateur obstacle course races. Those driving skills were about to come in handy.

Colleen zipped through the Island Sands development as fast

as her safety-conscious self would allow. She didn't want to be the cause of another death on their island. She rounded a corner and spotted the sedan up ahead. As the road straightened, she pushed the gas pedal and picked up speed. The gap between her and the sedan shortened.

As she raced down the straightaway, she noticed a herd of horses galloping alongside the road. She was afraid the horses would suddenly change direction and leap into traffic. Get out of the way, she silently ordered. But as she had feared, the lead horse took a sharp turn and darted across the road, the rest of the herd following behind. She hit her brakes hard and brought her SUV to a screeching stop as the last horse galloped across the road inches from her front bumper. Colleen watched helplessly as the sedan drove out of sight.

She flicked off the emergency lights, steered her vehicle back into its lane, snatched her phone, and dialed Bill. He needed to know about Pinky's nephew right away. She'd leave out the details of the high-speed chase. No need to get him upset about that now.

Bill picked up on the first ring. "You okay?"

"I'm fine," she said, "but I'm not sure Pinky is."

"What did you do?"

"It's what his nephew did. Where are you?" she asked, stopping at a stop sign.

"I'm pulling into Nell's with Myrtle."

"I'll meet you there. Take down this name. You'll want to run it through CODIS."

"What's this about?"

"I'll explain when I see you. The name's Max Cascio. He may also go by Sweet Boy Cascio. Got it?"

"Max 'Sweet Boy' Cascio," he said. "Got it."

"See you soon," she said and disconnected.

Colleen forced herself to drive the speed limit. She was anxious to get to Nell's and speak with Bill and Myrtle about what she had discovered but there was no use getting into an accident. The close call she had had with the horses was enough for one day.

She ran her conversation with Pinky over in her head. She was reasonably confident now that the man with the gun was Pinky's nephew. Had Pinky known about his activities in Corolla? It didn't sound like it from the way he had spoken of Max but then again, family members often helped other family members when they were in trouble with the law. Could Pinky be the stereotypical Italian gangster that Myrtle thought he was?

Though Colleen didn't have any reason to think Pinky was running anything but a legitimate real estate development business, she knew Myrtle wasn't the only one in Corolla who thought he had ties to the Mob. From the time he had arrived and began buying land, there had been rumors and speculation. Colleen had always chalked it up to a North versus South thing, but now she wasn't so sure.

One thing she was fairly certain of, however, was that Pinky's nephew had been up to shady dealings in Corolla. Still, she didn't have any proof. This was strictly a gut feeling. Pinky had said that Max had had "a tough go of it." She imagined that meant trouble with the law. But even if he hadn't broken the law, what type of man assaults his uncle while he's a guest in his home? At best, Max was an ungrateful nephew with an anger-management problem; at worst, he was a drug-dealing arsonist and killer.

Colleen wished she had gotten a look at Max before he had peeled away in the car. She wondered if Pinky had a photo or if a mug shot would come up when Bill had the FBI run Max Cascio's name through their database. If they got a photo, then they could get Ashley to identify Max . . . if they ever found out where Ashley and her family had vanished to after Miss Kennedy's death.

The thought of Ashley identifying a mug shot of Max Cascio, Max being arrested, and life in Corolla returning to normal lifted her spirits. But the feeling didn't last. As she was thinking about how nice it would be to have her life back and Myrtle out of her house, Colleen arrived at Nell's and discovered a crowd in the parking lot—with Myrtle and Little Bobby at its center.

Chapter 18

"*What the hell's wrong* with you, old man?" Colleen heard
Little Bobby shout as she jumped from her vehicle and swiftly
crossed the parking lot of Nell's Gift Shop and Rentals.

A small crowd of locals and fishermen had gathered near the
entrance to the store and Bobby, Myrtle, and Bill were in the
middle of it. Bill stood with his arms extended between Bobby
and the disguised Myrtle. He was doing his best to keep mother
and son apart but obviously had his hands full as Myrtle struggled to break free and go after her son. Nell hovered at the outer
perimeter with her hands over her mouth in shock.

"What's wrong with me? What's wrong with you?" Myrtle
yelled at Bobby, the fake mustache flapping with every animated
word.

"Who is this crazy man?" Bobby asked Bill, irritated.

Colleen wiggled past the crowd and into the center of the action. "He's my uncle," she said. "What seems to be the problem?"

"*He's* the problem," Bobby said, pointing at Myrtle.

Colleen shot Myrtle a stern look of disapproval, then glanced at Bill with alarm. They both knew that if they didn't get Myrtle away there really would be a problem.

"Seems your uncle Mitch doesn't approve of Bobby buying a Jet Ski from Nell," Bill said to Colleen.

"Those things are dangerous!" Myrtle shrieked.

"See what I mean?" Bobby said.

"Why don't you and I have a talk," Bill said to Myrtle, as he seized her firmly by the arm and led her away from Colleen and Bobby. The crowd pushed outward to allow Bill and Myrtle room to pass.

Colleen understood what Bill was up to. The best way to defuse the situation was to separate Myrtle and Bobby. She put her arm on Bobby's back. "Tell me what happened with my uncle," she said, gently turning Bobby so he no longer faced Myrtle.

"I was talking to Nellie about buying one of her Jet Skis and your uncle went ballistic. Called me a spoiled bum and an ungrateful child. Even told me my father was crying in heaven over how I'm behaving. Can you believe that?"

"Well, he is!" Myrtle yelled across the circle.

On the outside Colleen appeared calm and professional, but on the inside she wanted to slap Myrtle hard on her plump derriere. What did Myrtle think she was accomplishing by confronting Bobby? Did she want to blow her cover and the possibility of catching the person who tried to kill her over something as stupid as a Jet Ski?

"What Bobby says is true," Nellie said, stepping forward. "I don't know what's gotten into Mitch."

"I knew you were after me!" Myrtle screamed.

"Mitch, please. You're scaring me," Nellie said, tears in her eyes.

"Yeah? Well, y'all ain't seen nothing yet," Myrtle said, ripped off her sneaker, and threw it in Bobby's direction.

Nellie yelped and ducked behind Colleen. Murmurs rippled through the crowd. A few onlookers snapped photos on their cell phones. Colleen surveyed the growing crowd with concern. If they didn't get things settled quickly, the likelihood of Myrtle's disguise remaining intact was slim and the likelihood of the local press appearing great.

"That's assault," Bobby said. "That man should be arrested."

Cries of agreement came from the onlookers.

"Okay, people, that's enough," Bill said in a booming voice.

The crowd immediately quieted. Colleen had always been impressed by his ability to control a group.

"Nobody's getting arrested," he said to Bobby. "There's obviously been a misunderstanding."

"The only reason you're not arresting him is because he's Chief McCabe's uncle."

Before Bill or Colleen had a chance to refute Bobby's accusation, the news van appeared in the lot. She had to get Myrtle out quick before Myrtle opened her mouth and said something they'd all regret. She left Bobby and Nellie, snatched

Myrtle's shoe from the ground, and crossed to where Bill had Myrtle in a tight grip by the arm. "I think you need to go home, Uncle," she said through gritted teeth, and handed Myrtle her sneaker.

The news reporter and his cameraman shoved through the crowd.

"Oh good. The news. Now maybe somebody will listen to me," Myrtle said.

"We're always here to listen," the reporter said, pressing forward and signaling his cameraman to start recording.

"I know who killed Myrtle Crepe and Miss Kennedy," Myrtle said before Colleen could stop her.

Everyone gasped. Colleen and Bill silently groaned.

"Get her out of here," Bill said in an urgent whisper.

"What's your name, sir?" the reporter asked, thrusting the microphone toward Myrtle.

Colleen stepped between Myrtle and the reporter. "My uncle seems to be suffering from heat exhaustion. I'd like to get him home so he can rest. If you'll excuse us." She pushed Myrtle through an opening in the crowd and away from the reporter.

"Are the police going to investigate this man's suspicions?" Colleen heard the reporter ask as she marched Myrtle toward her SUV.

"Ouch! You're hurting me," said Myrtle, who struggled to keep up while wearing only one shoe.

Colleen yanked open the passenger-side door. "In the words of my uncle Mitch, you ain't seen nothing yet."

Myrtle opened her mouth to speak, then closed it again and

hopped into the SUV. Colleen slammed the door closed. Myrtle flinched. As she crossed around the front of the vehicle, Colleen looked back at the crowd. Some were still watching her and Myrtle but most were now directing their attention toward the reporter and cameraman.

"So you have no intention of following up with this lead, Sheriff?" Colleen heard the reporter ask as she jumped in the car.

Bill was now surrounded by the crowd and the media. "As you are well aware, we don't discuss ongoing investigations," he said.

She hated to leave Bill to deal with the press but it was the only option. She started the engine. "You better buckle up," she scowled at Myrtle. "It's going to be a bumpy ride."

Myrtle hurriedly buckled her seat belt as Colleen burned rubber. Colleen waited until Nell's shop had disappeared behind them before exploding at Myrtle. "A Jet Ski?" she said, trying to control her anger since she was driving. "You're going to blow everything over a Jet Ski?"

"They're dangerous."

"So is making a scene when you're in disguise because someone tried to murder you."

Colleen expected another feeble attempt at an excuse. When she didn't get one, she stole a look at Myrtle and saw her rubbing the sneaker's shoelace like rosary beads. Myrtle's eyes were welling and a tear dropped into her lap. Colleen sighed. It wouldn't do to have Myrtle upset and crying. If the plan that Colleen was formulating worked out, Myrtle was going to need her wits about her tonight.

"There's one good thing about what happened," Colleen said.

"We know Nellie's not the killer," Myrtle said with a sniffle.

Colleen turned to Myrtle, surprised. "But you thought Nellie wanted to get rid of you to get her hands on the documents."

Myrtle bowed her head. "I was wrong."

"I don't understand. What happened to make you change your mind?"

"I was talking to Nellie before . . . before the whole thing with Little Bobby happened. You know how she has a grandson in film school?"

Colleen nodded, not sure where Myrtle was going with this.

"She persuaded him to do a movie on the horses and he needs the documents for the film. It was going to be a surprise for me at Christmas. Nellie told Mitch that I would have liked it," Myrtle said. "Oh, I really put my foot in it."

"Or shoe," Colleen said, and chuckled despite everything.

Myrtle smiled impishly. Good, she thought. Time to tell Myrtle about her plan.

"You know, Myrtle, there is a silver lining in all of this."

"What's that?"

She paused to give her words added emphasis. "The trap has been set."

"What trap?"

"Well," she said, "if our killer sees the news, he'll pay us a visit tonight."

Myrtle pursed her lips, skeptical. "Why would he do that?"

"Because *my uncle* told the reporter he knows who killed

Myrtle Crepe and Miss Kennedy," Colleen said. "And *I* told them I was taking my uncle home to rest."

Myrtle's eyes widened with understanding.

"If all goes according to plan," Colleen said, "tonight we'll have company."

Chapter 19

"Police aren't talking about Mitch Connelly's claims that he knows the identity of the Corolla Killer, but one thing's for certain . . . this reporter will continue to work to get to the bottom of this. This is Doug Templeton for News Channel 4's Eye on Corolla."

Colleen clicked the television off. "The word is out," she said to Myrtle and Bill, who were sitting on the sofa.

"Looks like it," Myrtle said, crossing to the window and peeking through the curtains. "It'll be dark soon," she added, her nervousness apparent.

"Are you sure you want to do this?" Bill asked.

"I don't see that we have much choice."

"Rodney is staked out at the end of the drive behind the poplar grove. He'll give us the heads-up as soon as he spots the suspect approaching."

"Maybe we should call Special Agent Garcia."

"I did," he said.

"So why isn't he here?"

"Charlie confessed to more crimes," Colleen said. "Agent Garcia is busy questioning him."

"Oh, please," Myrtle said with an irritated wave. "Charles Nuckels wouldn't hurt anyone."

"At least not on purpose," Colleen said.

Bill shook his head. "It's hard to believe they're taking anything he says seriously."

"He must be getting a lot of attention," Colleen said. "Next he'll confess to kidnapping the Lindbergh baby."

Myrtle plopped back onto the sofa. Smokey crawled from underneath a chair and sprang into her lap. Colleen was actually relieved to see the Siamese jump on the usually forbidden lap of a guest. She hoped having Smokey with her would calm Myrtle's nerves.

"I'll take Sparky out back," Colleen said to Bill. "If we have any trouble from that side, he'll let us know."

"Good idea."

"Sparky, come," she said.

The Border collie leapt from his bed in the corner of the room and followed Colleen to the back of the house. As soon as she opened the door, he eagerly bounded onto the porch. The canine gazed at the water then back at Colleen.

"Not tonight, fella. You've got to keep guard."

Sparky flumped onto the porch. Colleen closed the door and rejoined Myrtle and Bill.

"You should probably get your disguise back on now, Mrs. Crepe," Bill said. "We don't know if our suspect will wait until dark to show. He certainly didn't with Rosemary Kennedy."

Myrtle lifted Smokey into her arms, left the room, and disappeared into the hall bathroom.

"Smokey can sit on the counter while Myrtle gets ready," Colleen and Bill heard Myrtle say to the cat before closing the bathroom door. There were more whispered sweet-nothings from Myrtle to the cat but Colleen couldn't make them out. Yes, it was going to take a long time to retrain Smokey.

"So now what?" she asked Bill.

"We wait."

She leaned against the wall, shoved her hands in her pockets, then yanked them out again and cracked her knuckles. She smiled at Bill sitting on the sofa. He gave her a weak smile back. "You want anything to drink?" she asked in an attempt to fill the silence.

"No, I'm fine."

She took a seat in the high-back chair and leaned closer to Bill. "You think Myrtle's okay with this?"

"Not really. But we're here with her."

The room fell quiet. Colleen listened to the clock ticking in the kitchen and the water running in the hall bathroom as Myrtle got ready. She and Bill were finally alone and she had no idea what to say to him. How had they come to this point? She had never been at a loss for words with him before. . . . Well, not until she and Myrtle had deceived him. She knew Bill was uneasy with their plan. It wasn't by the book. In fact, it was off the books. The only deputy he had informed about the situation was Rodney. Bill hated not having more backup.

Colleen wasn't thrilled with having to leave Jimmy and her guys in the dark. She had called Jimmy earlier to tell him she needed to take the night off due to her uncle's health but could tell by Jimmy's reaction that he knew she was lying and that her deception hurt his feelings. He thought she didn't trust him. But she did . . . with her life. She just didn't want to put any more people in danger.

Bill's walkie-talkie buzzed to life. "Come in, Bill, this is Rodney. Over."

Bill grabbed his walkie-talkie and hit the TALK button. "Rodney, this is Bill. Everything okay? Over."

"A car's approaching . . . looks like you've got company."

"Can you see the driver?"

"Hold on. They're driving kinda slow."

"Who is it, Rodney?" Bill asked, impatient.

"You're not going to believe . . . it's Nellie Byrd."

Colleen sensed another person in the room and discovered Myrtle standing in the doorway with Smokey in her arms.

"Did he say Nellie?" Myrtle asked.

"You sure it's Nellie?" Bill asked into the walkie-talkie.

"Yep. She just passed me."

"Thanks, Rodney," Bill said and released the button on the walkie-talkie.

"What's Nellie doing here?" Myrtle asked, squeezing Smokey tight.

Apparently, the squeeze was too tight and the cat jumped from Myrtle's arms and ran under the sofa.

"I guess we're going to find out," Colleen said. "Why don't you stay in the living room. Let me answer the door."

"I'll be right with you," Bill said to Colleen. "Just in case."

"Don't hurt her, Sheriff," Myrtle said.

"I won't. Now take a seat in the living room, Mrs. Crepe."

Colleen observed Myrtle head toward the living room, walking not as Mitch but as herself. "Myrtle?" she said.

Myrtle turned.

"Don't forget you're still Mitch Connelly."

Myrtle's eyebrows furrowed, puzzled.

"Your walk," Colleen said.

Myrtle paused a moment, thinking, then gave Colleen a thumbs-up and sauntered into the living room with her Mitch Connelly swagger.

A car pulled into the drive and stopped. An engine sputtered off; a door slammed; and footsteps were heard on the porch. Bill positioned himself in the corner behind the front door and sig-naled Colleen he was ready. They heard a light knock. Colleen waited a few seconds, then opened the door.

"Nellie? What are you doing here?" she asked, trying to appear as if all was normal.

"I'm sorry to disturb you, Chief McCabe, but I couldn't help worrying about Mitch. He was behaving so strangely today. Is he all right?"

"He's fine. Got a little too much sun is all."

"I made him a pie, if that's okay."

"It's perfect" came Myrtle's voice.

Colleen forced a smile and turned to find Myrtle standing in the foyer, having disobeyed Bill's request that she remain in the living room.

"I brought you strawberry rhubarb. It's one of my best," Nellie said and lifted the white box in her hands.

"How thoughtful of you," Myrtle said, strutting forward in her Mitch walk. "Colleen, why haven't you shown Miss Byrd in?"

Colleen frowned at Myrtle, then faked a smile and motioned for Nellie to enter. Nellie stepped inside. Colleen closed the door, revealing Bill standing along the wall.

Nellie jumped. "Sheriff Dorman, you startled me."

Colleen, Bill, and Myrtle stood silently in the foyer.

Nellie searched their faces. "Is something wrong?"

"I hope not," Bill said, serious. "Mind handing over the box?"

"Of course not," Nellie said and held the box out to him.

Bill made eye contact with Colleen and gestured toward the kitchen. They took the box into the kitchen and left Myrtle and Nellie watching from the foyer. Colleen opened a drawer, removed a pair of cooking scissors, and cut the string around the box. Bill gingerly lifted the lid. Colleen peered inside. The contents were indeed one of Nellie's famous strawberry rhubarb pies.

"Looks delicious," she said.

"I made it special for Mitch," Nellie said with a smile to Myrtle.

Bill found a knife, sliced into the pie, and raised a small piece to his nose. She watched Bill smell the piece and take a taste, puckering his lips several times. He was testing to see if Nellie had added any unusual, perhaps deadly, ingredients to the pie. Colleen crossed her fingers. Please let the pie be just that, she thought.

"That's some tasty strawberry rhubarb pie," he said.

Nellie beamed with pride. Colleen and Myrtle sighed with relief.

"Uncle, why don't you and Nellie come in the kitchen and have some pie?"

"That sounds fine," Myrtle said, adding a tad too much machismo to her voice. "After you, Miss Nellie."

Nellie took a seat at the table as Myrtle took out plates and silverware. When Colleen was certain Nellie wasn't paying attention to her and Bill, she motioned for him to follow her into the living room. She waited for Bill to join her and listened to Nellie and Myrtle making small talk in the kitchen before speaking.

"So," she said in a whisper, "Nellie's not the killer."

"We need to get her out of here. I don't want her in danger," he said.

"Agreed."

Bill's walkie-talkie buzzed to life. "Bill, it's Rodney. You there? Over."

"I'm here. What's up? Over."

"I spotted someone approaching waterside."

Colleen and Bill exchanged a quick look. If this was the killer, they needed to be sure Myrtle and Nellie were safe.

"Get an ID on the driver?" Bill asked.

"Got past me before I got a chance. Looks like a man, though."

Colleen and Bill heard the sound of some type of boat approaching from the dock side of the house.

"Thanks, Rodney," Bill said and clicked his walkie-talkie off.

"I'll take care of Myrtle and Nellie," she said, her heart racing.

"Keep them out of sight," he said, removed his gun from its holster, and crept toward the back door.

"I'm glad you like the pie," Nellie was saying as Colleen entered the kitchen.

Colleen nodded to Myrtle to indicate that someone was arriving. Just then Sparky began howling outside. Myrtle's eyes widened.

"Mitch, is something wrong?" Nellie asked.

"Nellie, I'm going to need you and Mitch to stay right here and be quiet, okay?" Colleen said, crossing to the windows and closing the blinds.

"What's going on?" Nellie asked.

"Please, listen to Colleen," Myrtle said.

Nellie nervously held on to Myrtle's hands. Colleen positioned herself in the doorway between the women and the back of the house. In the unlikely event the killer got past Bill, she was prepared to protect Myrtle and Nellie with her life. She hoped it wouldn't come to that.

Sparky barked loudly at the back door and then the barking ceased. Colleen's heart raced. Had the killer hurt her dog? She felt her muscles tense at the thought. The room fell silent.

Suddenly, there was a loud knock at the door. Myrtle and Nellie flinched. Colleen bent her knees, ready to spring into action. She heard the back door swing open, the sounds of a scuffle, and then a cry of pain. She leapt into the hall and found Bill yanking Little Bobby's arms behind his back. Sparky wagged his tail on the other side of the screen door, unharmed.

"What are *you* doing here?" Bobby asked Bill.

"I could ask you the same question," Bill said, clicking handcuffs on Bobby's wrists and taking him by the arm.

Colleen signaled Myrtle and Nellie to remain quiet.

"I came to see Chief McCabe's uncle," Bobby said, wincing from the tightness of Bill's grip.

"Why?" Colleen asked, stepping forward.

"Is this," Bobby said, indicating the handcuffs, "because of the fight I had with him?"

"Is it?" Bill asked.

Bobby eyed Colleen and Bill but said nothing.

"Not gonna talk? Perhaps you'd like to share your interest in Chief McCabe's uncle down at the station?" Bill said, jerking Bobby toward the front door.

"No, wait!"

Bill stopped. "Well?"

"This is going to sound crazy," Bobby said. "I don't even know how to say it."

"Bobby, if you've done something illegal—" Colleen said.

"What? No. It's nothing like that."

"Then what is it?" she asked.

"Today, when I saw your uncle throw his shoe at me, I got this idea. . . . I tried to put it out of my head but I couldn't. I kept thinking about it over and over and over."

"You're not making any sense," she said, now worried Bobby might need psychiatric care.

"It doesn't make any sense to me either. I mean, how could it?"

"How could what?" Bill asked.

"When Colleen's uncle threw that shoe at me today it reminded me so much of when my mother used to throw her shoe at Dad when she was mad at him. That's when I got this crazy idea."

Colleen and Bill exchanged looks. They knew what was coming next.

"You'll probably lock me up for saying this but, Chief McCabe, I think your uncle is my mother."

The room fell silent. Colleen glanced at Myrtle and Nellie in the kitchen. Both were wide-eyed but for different reasons.

"I told you it was crazy," Bobby said, his shoulders drooping. "I don't know why I even came here. I guess I just hoped . . ."

Bill eased his grip on Bobby's arm. "Let's have a seat in the living room."

As Bill led Bobby to the living room, Colleen retreated to the kitchen. "How are you two?" she asked Myrtle and Nellie.

"Poor Bobby," Nellie said.

"I want to talk to him," Myrtle said.

"I don't think that's a good idea," Colleen said.

"He's not the killer."

"Killer?" Nellie asked with surprise. "What killer?"

"We'll explain later," Colleen said. "Please, stay put. I'll be right back." She left the kitchen and joined Bill and Bobby in the living room.

"Bobby says he has something to tell you," Bill said as she entered.

"Oh?"

Bobby stared at his feet. Colleen looked at Bill for an answer. Bill shrugged.

She squatted in front of Bobby. "Does this have something to do with you selling your mother's house to Antonio Salvatore?"

Bobby gaped at Colleen. "How do you know that?"

"I saw you talking to him at his trailer."

She studied Bobby a moment. There was something more on his mind. "That's not what you wanted to tell me, is it?"

He shook his head. His eyes welled with tears and he said, "Burn burn burn."

"Speak up so we can hear you," Bill said.

Bobby sighed. "Burn burn burn," he said again and burst into tears.

Colleen stared at Bobby, perplexed. Wasn't that what Charlie had been chanting at Myrtle's memorial service? Why was Bobby saying that now? Then it hit her. It's what Crazy Charlie had been trying to tell her the night Myrtle's house exploded.

"Charlie heard you, saw you the night of the fire. That's why you got so angry at him at the memorial service."

"I didn't mean to set the fire; I was just so angry. Mother and I fought that night about selling the house. When she was at the fair I came back home. I hate living there. I lost it, started ripping things up. I don't remember doing it but I guess I knocked a candle over or something because when I got back in my car the next thing I knew, the house . . . the explosion . . . I panicked. Ran. I didn't know Mother had come home." Bobby broke down and sobbed.

Bill shook his head.

"And the kitchen window?" she asked. "Was that part of your vandalism when you got home?"

Bobby nodded and wept anew. "Don't you see? I can't go back to that house. It's the place where I killed . . . That's why I went to Mr. Salvatore. I've got to sell it."

"What about the motorcycle?" Bill asked, not fully convinced. "Seems like a peculiar way to grieve."

"I always wanted a bike. Mother wouldn't let me get one. Funny. Now I'd trade that bike and everything else just to have her back."

"It's a deal."

Colleen, Bill, and Bobby turned to see Myrtle in the living room entrance.

Nellie was at Myrtle's side a moment later. "Mitch, what's going on?" she asked.

"Go back to the kitchen, *Uncle*," Colleen said.

"I can't do this any longer," Myrtle said, tore the hat from her head, and stripped the mustache from her upper lip.

"Mother!" Bobby said, leaping from the sofa.

"Bobby!" Myrtle said and ran to her son.

"Oh!" Nellie gasped and clutched the wall.

Colleen groaned.

"Now, hold on one minute," Bill said, trying to pluck Myrtle's arms from around Bobby's plump waist.

"Myrtle? Is that really you?" Nellie asked in a daze as Colleen helped her to a chair.

"It's me, Nell," she said, still hugging Bobby.

"But . . . how? We're best friends."

"Remember I won the acting award senior year?"

Nellie stared at Myrtle in shock.

"I knew it was you," Bobby said and squeezed his mother until her feet came off the ground.

"Before we all get carried away with this reunion, there's still the matter of the murder of Rosemary Kennedy, the dead fisherman, and the drugs on the beach," Bill said, finally wrenching mother and son apart.

"Not to mention the identity of the person who did perish in that fire," Colleen added.

"That poor woman," Nellie said, still in shock.

"Oh, for heaven's sake. Little Bobby didn't have anything to do with those things and you all know it," Myrtle said in a huff.

"I may have accidentally caused that fire," Bobby said. "But I'm no drug-dealing murderer."

Colleen studied Bobby. She believed he was telling the truth; and if that was the case, the killer was still out there and perhaps on his way to the house. Bill must have been thinking the same thing because he grabbed his walkie-talkie.

"Stay right there," he said to Bobby, crossed to the foyer, and hit the button on his walkie-talkie. "Rodney, this is Bill. Over."

No response.

Bill clicked the TALK button again. "Rodney, are you there? Over."

Still nothing from the deputy. Colleen crossed to Bill and touched his arm. Rodney was their only lookout. Bill had chosen him not only because he was the best deputy but the strongest. If Rodney wasn't answering his walkie-talkie, something was dreadfully wrong.

Chapter 20

The only safe assumption is to assume the worst. Colleen had said this to her firefighters during training any number of times but never did it seem more relevant than it did now. With communication to Bill's deputy cut off there was a good chance that something terrible had happened to Rodney and that the killer was on his way to her house. Colleen hustled Myrtle and Nellie into the hallway away from the windows while Bill clicked off the foyer and porch lights and locked the front door.

"What's going on?" Nellie asked with a quiver in her voice.

Bill released Bobby from the handcuffs.

"Does this mean I'm free to go?" Bobby asked.

"No," Bill said.

"Please, tell me what's going on," Nellie said.

"We don't have much time," Colleen said. "We need to get you safe."

"Safe from what?"

"From the person who killed Miss Kennedy," Myrtle said.

Nellie swayed as if about to faint and Myrtle steadied her. "No time for dramatics, Nell," Myrtle said and placed Nellie's arm around her shoulders for support.

Sparky barked on the back porch. Everyone in the room fell silent. Bill crept toward the back door, his gun drawn. Bobby ducked into the kitchen. Colleen moved Myrtle and Nellie to the living room, against the wall, and positioned a chair in front of them for protection.

"Don't move," she said. She tiptoed across the room and peered down the hall to where Bill was tucked against the wall near the back door.

Bill turned the doorknob and opened the door. Colleen saw Sparky pacing on the shore near the dock. She squinted to see what Sparky was growling at. For a second she froze at the sight of her dock going up in flames. Then she blinked and the shock was gone.

"Fire," she said to Bill. "I'll get extinguishers."

"Wait until it's safe," he said but Colleen was already crossing to the kitchen.

She grabbed an extinguisher from the wall and an extra from the closet. "Come with me," she said to Bobby and handed him an extinguisher. She marched down the hall with Bobby on her heels. Ahead of her, Bill had stepped onto the porch and was scanning the grounds with his gun aimed in front of him. Sparky barked as the flames leapt down the dock toward the house. Colleen pushed open the door.

"I don't see anyone," Bill said.

"Good. Let's go." Colleen hurried past Bill with Bobby half walking, half running to keep up. Sparky ran to her as she reached the shore. "Good boy," she said, patting the dog's head. "Now stay."

Sparky whimpered but obeyed. She jogged down the dock toward the flames. Bobby struggled to keep up, the fire extinguisher in his hands throwing off his balance. She came to a stop a safe distance from the flames and waited for Bobby.

"Ever use one of these before?" she asked when a panting Bobby joined her.

Bobby shook his head.

"You're about to learn. Just remember the word 'pass.' Pull the pin, aim at the base of the fire, slowly squeeze the lever, and sweep from side to side," she coached and demonstrated. "Pull, aim, squeeze, sweep. Got it?"

Bobby set his jaw and straightened his shoulders. It was the first time she had seen him stand like a man in control. She faced the flames. "Pull the pin," she said, pulling her pin and releasing the locking mechanism. "Now aim the nozzle at the dock. Very little on the fire ground falls up."

She was pleased to see Bobby do exactly as instructed. "Good. Now squeeze the lever. Slowly." Extinguishing agent poured from the nozzles. "Move the extinguisher from side to side, like you're sweeping."

Colleen moved the nozzle back and forth, aiming at the base of the flames. Bobby did the same. They each took a section of the dock and edged foot by foot down the dock until the fire was completely out.

"You did great," she said as the charge on their extinguishers depleted.

Bobby grinned with pride. Colleen gave him a pat on the back. A Jet Ski bobbing in the water at the shore caught her eye and she was on alert again.

"What's that doing here?"

"I rented it at Nell's today; remember the scene in the parking lot?" Bobby said and hopped down to the shore a few feet below.

As Bobby waded into the water and secured the Jet Ski, Colleen strode up the dock toward the house. The sound of breaking glass from inside the house turned her walk into a sprint.

Sparky howled as Bill and Colleen ran to the house and up the porch steps. Bill cocked his gun, peered through the screen door, cracked it open, and slid inside. She and Sparky followed him in but Colleen pushed the dog back as they inched toward the living room.

"Where's the old man?" she heard a voice with a Brooklyn accent demand from the living room.

Bill edged sideways toward the living room entrance. Colleen clung to the opposite wall and out of sight. She and Bill moved forward until they saw the back of the intruder.

"We told you, we don't know about any old man," Myrtle said.

"You think I'm stupid? You think you can dress up in his clothes and fool me, you old hag?"

"That's enough," Myrtle said from the living room and a second later a shoe flew through the air, followed by the sound of breaking glass.

Bill and Colleen leapt forward and discovered the intruder rubbing his nose. On either side of him were broken lamps. Myrtle's shoes lay in the middle of the debris.

"Stop throwing shoes at me," the intruder said.

Colleen stared at the stranger, dumbfounded. How could it be that the person before her was none other than the handsome man who had smiled at her at the fireworks, the man she had seen at Myrtle's memorial service, the man who had helped her with her groceries at Food Lion? Was this man really responsible for the trouble in Corolla? Was he Pinky's ne'er-do-well nephew, Max "Sweet Boy" Cascio? And how could she have come that close to danger and not known it?

"You," she uttered.

The man sneered at Colleen. Gone was any hint of civility from their earlier encounter.

Bill's eyes narrowed. "You know this man?"

Colleen clenched her jaw, annoyed with herself for not having put two and two together. "Max, isn't it?" she said. "Or should I call you Sweet Boy?"

"How do you know my name?" Max asked, swinging his pistol toward her. "My uncle rat me out?"

"Drop the gun," Bill ordered, raising his revolver.

Sparky snarled and Colleen held his leash tight.

Max snatched Myrtle and swung her in front of him.

"Myrtle," Nellie said with a gasp.

"Don't do anything stupid, Max," Bill said, his gun leveled at Max's head.

Just then Bobby burst inside, down the hall, and into the living room. "Mother!" he cried, skidding to a stop when he saw Max with a gun pointed at Myrtle's temple.

"Back up," Max said, waving the gun wildly.

"Take it easy and everyone can walk away from this without getting hurt," Bill said.

"You bet I'm walking away," Max said, pressing the barrel even closer to Myrtle's temple. "Now back up, all of you, or I drop the old woman."

Nellie immediately moved away. Bobby raised a clenched fist. Colleen grabbed his arm and forced him to step away with her and Sparky.

"You, too, Sheriff," Max said, his eyes darting about the room.

Bill hesitated, then moved back. Max shuffled sideways with Myrtle in front of him.

"I'm not going anywhere with you, you hoodlum," Myrtle said and attempted to break free. Max yanked on her arm and she cried out in pain. "Monster," she said between gasps.

Colleen, Bill, Bobby, and Nellie watched helplessly as Max found his way to the front door and backed out of the house with Myrtle. Sparky yelped and jerked on his collar but Colleen held him firmly back. She didn't want him to get shot or endanger Myrtle.

"Are we just going to stand here?" Bobby asked as Max dragged Myrtle down the porch steps, threw her into the backseat of his sedan, and slipped into the driver's seat.

"No," Colleen said, her voice low.

The moment Max's vehicle pulled away from the house and

screeched down the driveway, Colleen and Bill sprang into action. Bill holstered his gun and dashed out the front door.

"Sparky, come," she said and ran after Bill.

"I'll take the water," Bobby said, slammed out the back door, and ran to his Jet Ski.

Colleen whipped open the door of her SUV and Sparky flew in. She hopped in, slammed the door closed, and started the engine.

Bill threw his vehicle in gear as Nellie appeared on the porch frantically waving her arms. "What about me?"

"You want me to take her?" Colleen asked Bill through her open window.

Bill shook his head and leaned out his window. "Get in," he said to Nellie.

Nellie hurried down the steps and into his car. He flipped on the flashing lights. His vehicle kicked up dirt as he sped down the driveway.

Colleen maneuvered her SUV and hit the gas. She glanced at Sparky, who was staring out the front windshield, his mouth open and tongue wagging.

Bill's vehicle pulled onto the side of the road up ahead. Colleen saw Rodney stumbling from the woods and rubbing his neck. As she approached, Rodney gave them a thumbs-up. Bill stopped near Rodney and Colleen slowed next to Bill.

"You okay?" Bill asked his deputy.

"I'll be fine. Go on," Rodney said and waved them on.

Bill turned to Colleen. "Head toward Lighthouse. I'll see if I can't block off Ocean Trail and send him back your way."

She nodded and Bill took off down the road with his lights flashing and siren blaring. Sparky whined at the sound and rotated in a circle on the passenger seat.

"Hang on," she said to the dog and peeled out.

Colleen's cell phone rang. She answered without checking the number.

"Chief, it's Bobby Crepe" came the screaming voice at the other end.

Colleen heard the sound of a loud motor and water splashing in the background. "Where are you?"

"I'm tracking that criminal from Raccoon Bay. I can't see him now because of the trees but he was heading down Ocean Trail. I'm gonna try and beat him down the island and cut him off when I get to the sound."

"I don't think you'll have enough time to dock and cut him off."

"Who said anything about docking?"

Colleen's eyebrows furrowed. How did Bobby expect to cut Max off if he didn't dock and get a car? In a second, the answer hit her. "Bobby! You can't ground the Jet Ski. You'll get yourself killed."

"There's a ramp at Shad. It's worth a try. Look after my mother."

The connection went dead. She rode in silence for a moment, then speed-dialed. Bill picked up on the first ring.

"Bill. Listen. Bobby says Max is headed down Ocean Trail. He's going to try and cut Max off by grounding his Jet Ski."

"That's impossible. He'll get himself killed."

"That's what I said. Any way we can stop him?"

"Wish we could, but he's got a pretty good lead on us from the water."

"Then I'll call the station and send the guys over. If he tries it, there will be EMTs at the ready."

"And that should force Max down Corolla Drive."

"I'll have the guys block Corolla with the engine. Then we should have him," she said and disconnected.

She hit speed-dial for the station. After two rings Jimmy picked up. "Jimmy? Chief McCabe."

"What's up, Chief?"

"Bill and I are chasing down a suspect in Miss Kennedy's murder. Can you get the guys to pull the engine across Corolla Drive? Bobby Crepe and Bill are going to force him down that way."

"Say that again," Jimmy said, shock in his voice.

"I'll explain later. Just get the EMTs to the intersection of Shad and Ocean Trail and the engine out on Corolla. Got it?"

"Right away, Chief."

Colleen hung up and raced down Ocean Trail. She wondered how Myrtle was doing with Max. Then again, the better question might be how Max was doing with Myrtle. She pictured Myrtle bonking Max on the head and shrieking while he tried to drive. Max had likely gotten more than he bargained for in grabbing Myrtle.

Colleen decreased her speed as flashing lights from the ambulance came into view on the road up ahead. She hoped her team had made it to Shad Street before Bobby attempted his daredevil Jet Ski jump. Sparky barked in recognition at the ambulance as they drew closer. She decelerated and one of the EMTs jogged to the road to meet her.

"Hey, Chief," the EMT said as Colleen braked on the shoulder. "Where's Bobby Crepe?"

"On the stretcher. He'll be okay, the fool."

"The engine out on Corolla Drive?"

"Yeah. But I saw Bill chase the suspect down Whalehead."

"Damn," she said under her breath.

The EMT's eyes widened. Colleen didn't typically swear around her employees. "Good work," she said and drove away from the scene.

Colleen turned onto Shad Street. If Max went down Whalehead instead of Corolla Drive, he must have seen the engine blocking the road. What should she do? Corolla, Whalehead, and Lighthouse Drives ran parallel to one another and were populated with vacationers in beach houses. She couldn't speed down the streets without risking hitting someone. The situation reminded her of when she was a kid and her mother sent her to get a forgotten item in the grocery store. Colleen would find the item but have a hard time locating her mother as she ran along the aisles, sometimes just missing her when each was blocked by the aisle end. She continued down Shad until she reached the point where it dead-ended at the beach and intersected with Lighthouse Drive. She tapped the steering wheel, worried.

Sparky yipped out the passenger-side window. Colleen scanned Lighthouse Drive and saw headlights rapidly approaching, followed by flashing police lights. She grinned with admiration. True to his word, Bill had forced Max back the way he had come. She threw her vehicle into gear and backed it up so it blocked access to the exit via Shad Street. Now the only way Max could turn when he reached the end of Lighthouse Drive was right, and that led to a dead end on the beach.

She glanced out the window and saw the lights quickly approaching. Too quickly. She flung open her door and leapt from her SUV. "Sparky, come," she said and slapped her thigh. The dog bounced out the driver's side and followed her as she ran away at full speed. Seconds later, Colleen heard the sound of metal slamming metal and knew that Max had rammed her SUV. Max reversed the sedan and sped right in the direction of the beach. We've got you now, she thought, and sprinted toward the beach with Sparky.

Bill skidded to a stop and jumped from his vehicle, lights still flashing. Nellie gingerly opened the back door of Bill's SUV, slid out, and hurried toward the beach.

Colleen pumped her arms up the short hill at the end of Shad Street and stopped short when she reached the crest. The charcoal-colored sedan sat stuck in the sand a few yards away with the driver's-side door open.

Bill caught up to Colleen as she cautiously approached the car. He signaled her to wait and unholstered his gun.

Nellie plodded through the sand several yards behind them. "Myrtle?" she said, biting back tears.

Colleen, Bill, and Nellie held their collective breath. The back door opened with a squeak and Myrtle staggered from the vehicle. "That guy won't bother *me* again," she said, brandishing a belt in her hand.

"Oh, Myrtle," Nellie said, tears in her eyes, and stumbled through the soft sand toward her best friend.

Colleen scanned the beach as Bill took Myrtle's arm and helped her walk to Nellie. At dusk the beaches were fairly deserted. There was a couple kissing on a blanket, a family playing badminton, and a man hiking up the beach. Colleen squinted at the man. Despite his rather casual pace, he seemed overdressed for an evening's stroll on the beach. "Bill," she said. "Up the beach."

Colleen pointed to the man. She and Bill dashed to the firmer sand at the shoreline. Once near the water, Colleen picked up speed. Sparky ran beside her, his fur getting wet from the splashing waves.

Ahead, Max turned, spotted Colleen and Bill, and bolted. She pumped her arms harder and shot forward. She spied a herd of wild horses up the beach from Max and glanced at Sparky running beside her.

"Sparky, herd the horses!"

It was what the Border collie had been waiting for. Sparky took off running, breaking away from Colleen and closing the gap on Max. Max saw the dog gaining on him and began zigzagging up the beach. Sparky quickly reached and then passed Max, racing straight for the horses. Max looked back at her and smirked. *He thinks I sent Sparky after him and now he's safe*, Colleen thought. She grinned. Max had no idea what was about to happen to him . . . if her plan worked.

She continued at a strong pace, thankful for all the early mornings she had forced herself to go jogging rather than get a few extra minutes of sleep. She stole a look behind her and saw Bill dropping back. He waved for her to keep going. She pushed forward despite the burn she felt in her calf muscles.

Sparky approached the horses from behind and nipped at their heels. The horses whipped their tails and attempted to move away from the pesky canine. The dog bent his head low, raised his haunches, salivated, and snapped at the heels of any horse that got too far from the group. Despite the danger of being kicked, Sparky was enjoying himself.

Colleen knew by the horses' movements that they were growing increasingly annoyed with Sparky's persistent nipping. If he kept it up, he would have the horses worked into an irritated frenzy, something she was counting on.

Max scampered up the beach toward the horses with Colleen right behind him. Max saw her closing the distance between them and waved his gun. She reduced her speed and Bill caught up to her.

"You see that?" she said between breaths.

"Uh-huh," Bill said, sucking in air.

"I hope he fires it."

Bill stared at her as if she was insane. "Not at us," she said. "To spook the horses."

Max reached the horses. He tried darting first left, then right around the herd. But as Colleen had hoped, Sparky had succeeded in working them into a fit of irritation and some were rearing up in an attempt to stop the dog from nipping at them. Frustrated, Max raised his gun in the air and fired. At that moment, Colleen knew the footrace was over for Max "Sweet Boy" Cascio.

At the sound of the gunfire, the horses recoiled and neighed. Max was surrounded by a mass of sweating, snorting steeds. He fell to his knees and raised his arms over his head to shield himself from being trampled. Sparky barked at the addition of Max to the horse mix.

Colleen and Bill reached the herd and staggered to a stop, exhausted. "Sparky, heel," she said.

Sparky cocked his head at her. His tongue hung out of his mouth and she could swear he was smiling. The horses bolted up the beach, leaving Max slumped in the sand.

Bill stepped forward, still catching his breath, and seized Max by the arm. "Max Cascio, you're under arrest," he said, lifting Max to his feet and slapping cuffs on his wrists.

Sparky barked at Max as he rose. "Good job," Colleen said and rubbed Sparky's ears.

Bill gazed at her. "Yes, good job," he said, pointedly.

Colleen smiled. You're welcome, she thought.

Chapter 21

Colleen observed the swarm of reporters gathered outside the sheriff's department with awe. She had never seen so much press on their island. All the major networks had sent their mainland crime reporters to cover the conference that Bill and Special Agent Garcia had called the morning after the arrest of Max "Sweet Boy" Cascio. She almost felt sorry for Corolla's local reporter, who was obviously miffed that the story was no longer exclusively his.

Bill and Garcia stood at the podium with a dozen or so microphones pointed at them like needles to two magnets. Colleen was positioned to the side of the podium with Rodney. She had been asked to attend the press conference in case the reporters had any questions but Garcia had made it clear to her last night that the less she said the better. She had wholeheartedly agreed.

"Thank you for coming," Garcia said, immediately quieting

the press. "As you all know, last night we arrested Maximillian Anthony Cascio, also known as Max 'Sweet Boy' Cascio, a native of Brooklyn, New York, for heroin trafficking and the murders of Rosemary Kennedy and Frank Bremer. At this time, we suspect Mr. Bremer witnessed and interrupted a drug transaction involving Mr. Cascio and a Colombian courier while fishing off the shore of North Carolina. We now know that Mr. Cascio brutally murdered Mr. Bremer, burned his boat and body to cover up his crime, and buried the heroin in the dunes with the intention of retrieving it later. Ms. Kennedy was subsequently murdered after working with an eyewitness on a police sketch. I should note that Mr. Cascio has a long record of criminal behavior and was considered armed and dangerous. In light of that fact and in conjunction with local law enforcement, we placed Myrtle Crepe into protective custody when we believed an attempt was made on her life. It appears that Mr. Cascio acted alone in the murders of Ms. Kennedy and Mr. Bremer. DEA is currently working with the Colombian government to investigate the individuals who sold the heroin to Mr. Cascio for distribution within the United States. I'd like to thank Sheriff William Dorman for his cooperation with our investigation and the vital information he provided to the FBI and DEA."

Colleen smiled as the crowd, particularly locals, applauded Bill. He acknowledged the crowd with a brief wave.

"At this time, we'll take a few questions," Garcia said.

"You mentioned Myrtle Crepe was in protective custody. Where has she been all this time?" one reporter asked.

Colleen eyed Myrtle and Nellie, who were listening nearby from inside Nellie's car.

"Ms. Crepe was kept in a safe house."

"Where?" asked another reporter.

"If I told you, it wouldn't be a safe house," Agent Garcia said, and laughter rippled through the crowd.

"Speaking of Ms. Crepe, why isn't Mr. Cascio being charged with the arson of her home and the murder of Edna Daisey?"

Agent Garcia glanced at Colleen before answering. "A thorough investigation of the incident by Fire Chief McCabe and her department determined the cause of the fire to be accidental. The coroner's report indicates that Edna Daisey, the victim found in the fire at the Crepe home, died from myocardial infarction, not the fire. Her death appears unrelated to this case."

Myrtle and Nellie shook their heads. Despite Myrtle's feud with Edna over the Lighthouse Wild Horse Preservation Society, Myrtle hadn't wanted Edna dead—not really.

It had taken a bit of work, but Colleen had learned from Edna's best friend Ruby that on the Fourth of July Edna had called Ruby while Ruby was on a two-week Alaskan cruise. Edna had told Ruby of her plan to steal the Lighthouse Wild Horse Preservation Society records while Myrtle was at the fair. Having heard Edna's tirades before and annoyed that Edna had called her while on vacation, Ruby hadn't taken Edna's scheme too seriously. Colleen and Ruby suspected that Little Bobby's surprise arrival home and violent outburst had startled Edna enough to stress her enlarged heart and led to the cardiac arrest. Ruby's prolonged vacation meant nobody had noticed Edna missing, and the disfigurement caused by the fire had delayed the coroner's identification of the body. Even though Bobby had never seen Edna in the house, he still felt somewhat responsible. The bottom line was that Edna's own behavior, not the fire, had led to her death. Colleen sighed. Sometimes it's better to let things go.

"You mentioned an eyewitness worked with Ms. Kennedy. Where is that eyewitness now?" Colleen heard a reporter ask and returned her attention to the press conference.

"With relatives in Raleigh," Garcia said.

"Did the eyewitness identify Mr. Cascio from a mug shot?"

"Yes."

"What about Charles Nuckels? Didn't he confess to the very same crimes you are now arresting Mr. Cascio for?"

"I'll take that one," Bill said, stepping in. "As those of you who are part of our community know, Charlie Nuckels has a vivid imagination." A few giggles were heard from the crowd. "I'm afraid Charlie let that imagination get the best of him. He now understands the seriousness of the charges and has admitted that he had no part in the crimes mentioned."

"What about Antonio Salvatore's part? Isn't he Mr. Cascio's uncle?"

"He is," Bill said. "But there's no indication that he had any knowledge of what his nephew was up to in Corolla. I ask that you respect Mr. Salvatore's privacy as you would any member of our community. After all, who among us doesn't have family or past relationships we'd rather kept private?"

Colleen studied Bill, surprised. His answer was unexpected

given how he felt about Pinky. She was impressed by his professionalism. But then something in her gut made her wonder if his response didn't come more from personal experience or feelings. Did Bill have something or someone he wanted kept private? Did it have anything to do with her? Stop it, she scolded herself. Not everything is about you and not everyone has ulterior motives. She pushed the questions from her mind.

"Thank you for coming. That will be all the questions for now," Garcia said, officially ending the press conference.

Reporters called after Garcia as he entered the sheriff's department building, then hurried to do their stand-ups for their news reports. Bill joined Colleen and Rodney.

"Nice job," Rodney said. "Glad I didn't have to do it."

"Why don't you head in, Rodney? We've got a meeting with Agent Garcia in five minutes."

"Nice working with you, Chief McCabe," Rodney said and left Colleen and Bill alone.

"How are you holding up?" she asked once Rodney was gone.

"I hate the press. And you?"

"I'm a little sore from yesterday but otherwise fine."

"Hey, Chief," Bobby said to her as he limped toward them. "Hey, Sheriff Dorman."

Bill shook his head. "I can't believe you're okay after that stunt you pulled."

"It was nothing," Bobby said with pride.

"Really?" she asked with raised brows and a smile.

"Well, I am a little bruised," Bobby said touching his bandaged cheek. "But nothing major."

Colleen stole a glance at Myrtle and Nellie. "So how are things with you and Myrtle?"

"We had a long talk. Mother is going to stay with Miss Byrd while the house is repaired and I'm going to get my own place."

"I think it's for the best," she said with a wink. "So, are you still coming to the orientation meeting at the station?"

"Definitely," Bobby said, his mood brightening. "Monday in two weeks, right?"

"That's right."

"Great. I'll see you then. Bye, Sheriff," he said, crossed the lot, and mounted his motorcycle.

"What was that all about?" Bill asked.

Colleen grinned. "After everything that has happened, Bobby's thinking of becoming a firefighter."

Bill raised his brows in surprise and he and Colleen burst out laughing.

"What's so funny?" Myrtle said through the passenger window as Nellie pulled next to them in her Buick.

"Oh, nothing," Colleen said. "I see you're letting Nellie drive for a change," she added, teasing Myrtle.

"It was time," Myrtle said with a shrug.

"Thirty years. I'd say it was time," Nellie said with a roll of the eyes.

Colleen and Bill chuckled.

"You two are certainly happy today," Myrtle said.

"You should be, too. You don't have to stay with me anymore."

Myrtle and Nellie grew quiet.

"I'm gonna miss Smokey," Myrtle said after a pause.

"And I'm gonna miss Mitch," Nellie said.

"Maybe Mitch can visit his niece and Smokey again sometime," Myrtle said.

"Really?" Nellie asked, looking with hope into Myrtle's eyes.

"Of course, it's up to Colleen. Uncle Mitch wouldn't want to visit without being invited."

Colleen couldn't believe the bizarre charade that was playing out between the two old friends. Even more unbelievable was that she found herself playing along. "Yeah, sure, maybe Uncle Mitch can visit sometime."

"That's wonderful," Nellie said, smiling at Myrtle.

Bill stared at her in disbelief. Colleen shrugged. There was no rational explanation for why she had agreed to indulge the old women's fantasy other than it seemed to make them both happy.

"You want to join us for pancakes?" Myrtle asked Colleen and Bill, her mood now bright.

"Thanks, but I've got a meeting with Agent Garcia," Bill said.

"And I need to get to the station. There's a lot to do since I was tied up with the investigation."

"Suit yourself," Myrtle said. "Okay, Nell, let's hit the road."

Nellie saluted, gunned the engine, and drove from the lot.

Colleen watched the Buick disappear. "What just happened?"

"You lost your mind," Bill said.

She grinned. "I think you're right. But it sure feels good." She checked the time. "I should let you get to your meeting."

Bill lingered.

"Something else on your mind?" she asked.

He took a breath and straightened his back. "I was wondering . . . what are you doing tonight?"

She felt the temperature rise several degrees. Was Bill really asking her out?

"I thought we could catch a movie, relax after everything that's happened," he added.

Before Colleen had a chance to answer, his phone rang. He checked the number and his cheeks flushed red. It rang several more times.

"Aren't you going to get that?" she asked.

"Uh, yeah, could you hold on a minute?" He turned his back and walked a short distance away before she could answer.

Colleen strained to hear what Bill was saying. All she could make out was "Wow . . . okay . . . in Corolla?" and then her phone rang. She looked at the number. It was the station. She hit the ANSWER button. "What's up, Jimmy?" she asked while keeping an eye on Bill.

"Mr. Salvatore," Jimmy said. "Seems he's threatening to burn debris if you don't come by."

Colleen turned her focus from Bill to her conversation with Jimmy. "But he's not actually burning debris?"

"Nope."

She smiled. Threatening to burn debris and actually burning it were two different things. Could she be making progress with Pinky? It was a baby step, but she'd accept it.

"You want me to go out there?" Jimmy asked.

"No. If he calls again, tell him I'm on my way. Thanks." Colleen returned her phone to her pocket and turned to find Bill stand-ing next to her, his call having obviously ended.

"Everything okay?" he asked.

"Yeah, it was Jimmy," she said, keeping her impending visit to Pinky to herself. "And you?" she said, gesturing to the phone in Bill's hand.

"Just someone I haven't heard from in a while," he said. "So where were we?"

Colleen studied Bill a moment, trying to remember what they had been talking about before the calls. She had never seen him flustered like he was by that phone call. It almost made her forget that he had asked her to the movies. Almost.

"I believe you were asking me about my plans for tonight," she said. "I have none."

Rodney opened the front door of the sheriff's department building. "Hey, boss, everyone's waiting," he said to Bill.

Bill waved to Rodney, then turned to Colleen. "I'll see you later then?"

She grinned. "Absolutely."

His eyes wrinkled in a smile behind his sunglasses. She had missed that smile. He turned away and she crossed the lot to her SUV. She slid into her vehicle, watched Bill enter the building, and let out a satisfied sigh. All was right in the world again.

Colleen drove toward Pinky's development with the windows down. The salty ocean breeze whipped her hair around her face and the summer sun warmed her left forearm as it rested on the window frame. She rounded a corner and spotted a mare and her foal grazing on vegetation near a vacation home. The vacationers were gathered on the balcony of the house taking pictures. She slowed to watch the mother with her baby. As she passed, the foal nuzzled its mother and she heard a chorus of "aws" from the onlookers. Colleen beamed. Today was going to be a glorious, blue-sky day in Corolla.